POTION PROBLEMS

ALSO BY CINDY CALLAGHAN

Just Add Magic

Lost in London

Lost in Paris

Lost in Rome

Lost in Ireland (formerly titled *Lucky Me*)

Lost in Hollywood

Sydney Mackenzie Knocks 'Em Dead

JUST ADD MAGIC

POTION PROBLEMS

CINDY CALLAGHAN

ALADDIN

New York   London   Toronto   Sydney   New Delhi

ALADDIN

An imprint of Simon & Schuster Children's Publishing Division

1230 Avenue of the Americas, New York, New York 10020

First Aladdin paperback edition August 2018

Text copyright © 2018 by Cindy Callaghan

Cover illustration copyright © 2018 by Annabelle Metayer

Also available in an Aladdin hardcover edition.

All rights reserved, including the right of reproduction in whole or in part in any form.

ALADDIN and related logo are registered trademarks of Simon & Schuster, Inc.

For information about special discounts for bulk purchases, please contact Simon & Schuster Special Sales at 1-866-506-1949 or business@simonandschuster.com.

The Simon & Schuster Speakers Bureau can bring authors to your live event. For more information or to book an event, contact the Simon & Schuster Speakers Bureau at 1-866-248-3049 or visit our website at www.simonspeakers.com.

Book designed by Nina Simoneaux

The illustrations for this book were rendered digitally.

The text of this book was set in Lomba Book.

Manufactured in the United States of America 0718 OFF

10 9 8 7 6 5 4 3 2 1

The Library of Congress has cataloged the hardcover edition as follows:

Names: Callaghan, Cindy, author.

Title: Potion problems / by Cindy Callaghan.

Description: First Aladdin hardcover edition. | New York : Aladdin, 2018.

Series: Just add magic ; 2 | Identifiers: LCCN 2018001761 | ISBN 9781534417403 (hc)

ISBN 9781534417410 (pbk) | ISBN 9781534417427 (eBook)

Subjects: BISAC: JUVENILE FICTION / Cooking & Food. | JUVENILE FICTION / Social Issues / Friendship. | JUVENILE FICTION / Girls & Women. |

Classification: LCC PZ7.C12926 Po 2018 | DDC [Fic—dc23]

LC record available at https://lccn.loc.gov/2018001761

If I had a secret club, Tricia and Maria would HAVE TO
be in it with me. This book is for them with great
appreciation for our oh so many years of eating dessert
first and living life with lots of spice!

1

It All Starts with a Problemo

Question: Why was I, Kelly Quinn, jumping on the bed late at night, over and over again? Was it: Exercise? A relaxation technique? A way to digest my dinner?

Answer: *None of the above.*

There was a very special book—a Secret Recipe Book—that I kept hidden in the tiles above my bed. And the only way to access it was this jumping situation.

I jumped again and reached into the ceiling for the Secret Recipe Book like I had so many times before.

Except this time, it wasn't there.

I texted my besties, Hannah Hernandez and Darbie O'Brien immediately.

Do either of you have it?

It? Darbie texted back, followed immediately after

by, **The pox?** Before I could reply, she added, **Small Pox or Chicken Pox?** I was almost ready to send my response when a third text came in from her: **Doesn't matter. I don't have either.**

Hannah wrote, **The Book, Darb. You took it home with you last night.**

Guilty, Darbie wrote. **It's right—**

Right where? I wrote. At this point I was sweating. This was no ordinary book.

She didn't respond for too many seconds. . . .

A few weeks ago, on the last day of summer vacation, Darbie and Hannah and I found the Secret Recipe Book hidden in my attic.

Who am I? Kelly Quinn, seventh grader, average/mediocre soccer player, and lover of all things cooking.

What's the Secret Recipe Book? It's a bunch of handwritten recipes taped within the pages of an old *World Book Encyclopedia, Volume T.* With the Book, we formed a secret cooking club and made the recipes, which called for some pretty unusual ingredients that we could only get from one local store: La Cocina.

Weird things happened to the people who ate the food (a.k.a. potions), and also to us. Seems that potioning someone comes with a price, like a payback. It's called the Law of Returns. So any time we make a potion, the person who adds the special ingredient gets a Return, which is bad luck.

Darbie? I wrote again.

She returned, **Problemo**.

Problemos with the Secret Recipe Book were not good.

2

The Darbie Decimal System

I paced around my kitchen later that evening. Darbie sat on a bar stool, more interested in stirring a yogurt with a pretzel stick than in answering Hannah's questions.

"Where did you leave it?" Hannah asked.

"In my house."

"That's good. Good start," Hannah said. "Now, can you be more specific?"

"In my room."

Hannah blew her bangs out of her face and took the yogurt away from Darbie, who instantly pouted. I knew from experience that taking food from Darbie was *the opposite* of what you should do to get her cooperation—her mind didn't work without a constant infusion of sugar. Actually, it sometimes didn't work even with the influx of sugar.

"Here, Darbie." I handed her a family-size bag of peanut M&M's after reaching in and taking a few out for myself.

Darbie's pout reversed. "Thanks, Kell. You know me so well." She took a handful from the bag, plucked out the orange ones, and put the others back in.

"Do you have to touch them all?" Hannah asked.

I stood between them, facing Darbie, and asked her, "Where in your room?"

She popped an orange M&M and looked up into her brain for details. "On my collection stack. You know it's as tall as me?"

"That's the pile where you store stuff you've found but don't have any place to put, right?"

"*Yet*," she explained. "I don't have a place to put it *yet*, but I will once everything is cataloged and sorted. You've heard of the Dewey decimal system? I'm going to make my own—the Darbie decimal system. But that's just a working title, and there won't be any decimals or math. Whatcha think?"

Hannah tried to get her back on track. "But the Book wasn't on or in your pile this morning?"

"Definitely not. I checked." Darbie chomped on more

M&M's. "In fact, now that I think about it, the Secret Recipe Book wasn't the only thing missing, because the pile was quite a bit shorter than me this morning. Or maybe I got a lot taller overnight. You know, like a growth spurt."

"I don't think those happen overnight," I said.

There was a knock on the back door, which was not so much a knock, but more an angry bang that we all recognized.

"Ugh," Darbie said.

I went to the door, but, before opening it, said to the girls, "Not a word about the Book. You know how she is."

Our neighbor and frenemy, Charlotte, stepped inside without bothering with hello. "You keep all of your guests waiting outside like that, Kelly Quinn?"

"You're not exactly a guest," I said. "You're a neighbor."

"And uninvited," Hannah added.

"Now who's not being neighborly?" Charlotte propped her hands on her hips. "Is this a meeting of the secret cooking club?"

Charlotte had recently found out about the club and thought it was the funniest thing in the world. Then she told everyone about it. So much for secret.

Hannah asked, "Does it look like we're cooking?"

Charlotte must not have felt like mocking us at this moment, which was rare. Instead she said, "I'm here on official student council business. I'm collecting gently used books for the annual book drive, and I've come to pick up what you have. I stress *gently*, not like the ones we got from Darbie's house."

"That's what was missing from my pile! My books!"

"The books," I confirmed.

"The Book," Hannah said.

"My mom donated the book," Darbie whispered.

"Is there an echo in here?" Charlotte asked. "Most of the books from Darbie's house were in such bad shape we had to put them straight into recycling. I hope the Quinns can step up the quality."

I moved to the door and opened it. "I'll bring some over later." Charlotte didn't move toward the door. I added, "Later today."

Charlotte looked at Darbie, who was sorting M&M's and eating only orange ones.

"You know they all taste the same."

"Not true," Darbie said. "Watch." She got one of each color M&M and set them on the kitchen counter, then she slipped a cloth napkin from under a bowl of fruit. "Blindfold me, Kell."

I tied the napkin around her head so she couldn't see.

"Wait." She lifted it and peered at Charlotte. "A bet?"

"Oh, for sure," Charlotte said. "If you can name all the colors by taste, I'll let you be captain at the next soccer practice. And if you can't—"

"Deal!" Darbie pulled the napkin back down and stuck out her hand.

I put in a yellow.

Darbie ate it.

Next I handed her blue, then red, green, brown, and orange.

When she was done, she lifted the blindfold.

Charlotte's hands found her hips again. "Exactly the same, aren't they?"

Darbie said, "First yellow, then blue, red, green, brown, and orange." To me she said, "You saved the best for last. Thanks, Kell."

"No way. Oh come on." She looked at me. "Kelly Samantha Quinn, you cheated." The only person besides Charlotte who has ever used my middle name is my mother, because it's the same as hers. Charlotte didn't have a reason except to irritate me. "Darbie knew what order you were putting those M&M's in."

"I did not," Darbie said. "And I resent the implication that I can't tell the difference between the taste of M&M's."

Charlotte moved toward the door. "I'll show myself out."

"Oh, one more thing," I said. "I'm just curious, because we have tons of old newspapers to get rid of, what do you do with your recycling?"

"We put it in the Dumpster behind Sam's iScream, like everyone else in town."

"Right," I said. "Well, we're going there later today to drop the newspapers, so we could bring your recycling over at the same time. You know, to be neighborly."

"That's so kind of you, Kelly. I'll tell my mom you're coming to get it." She went to close the door, but then reopened it and stuck her head back in. "Oh, but if you're looking for a *World Book Encyclopedia* with a Secret Recipe Book inside, you won't find it there. No, I'm keeping that for myself. Ta, girls." She pulled the door shut and gave a wiggly-fingered wave through the window, a devilish grin on her face.

"*Problemo,*" Darbie said.

"*Mucho,*" Hannah said.

"*Grande,*" I agreed.

3

A Little Hypnosis, Anyone?

hat we can do?" I asked.

"What if she makes something?" Hannah asked.

"We'd be frogs, for sure. She would turn us into frogs before she did anything else," Darbie said. "I know how her evil mind works, and that's what she'd do first."

"I agree," I said. "But she hasn't yet, so she must just want to hold it for ransom, right?"

"Fat chance," Hannah said.

Honk.

"That's my mom," Darbie said.

Honk.

"And there's my dad," Hannah said.

I said, "Think about how we'll get that book back, and we'll make a plan on the bus tomorrow morning."

"You know, if you want me to think, I'm going to need . . ." Darbie nodded at the bag of M&M's.

"Fine." I handed it to her. "Take it with you."

"Thanks, Kell. I'll bring back the non-orange ones."

"That's okay. They're all yours."

The next morning, I ran to catch the bus, got on and wiggled myself into a seat between Hannah and Darbie, and caught my breath.

"Running late?" Hannah asked.

"I stopped at Mrs. Silvers's house to scoop the poop."

"Is she still complaining about that?" Darbie asked.

Mrs. Silvers was our neighbor across the street. She had been ridiculously mean until she got her knee replaced. We even referred to her as "the witch." But since the surgery, she's like a whole new person.

"No," I said. "I just wanted to. I think she's changed, and I want to help her out, even if it isn't from my dog."

"You and her are like . . . BFFs now?" Hannah asked.

"We're getting along better than ever, actually. She even gave me this." I showed them the flyer for the Felice Foudini Recipe Challenge. Felice Foudini is this amazing

TV chef. I was on her show once when I was a kid. She probably doesn't remember me, but I'll never forget.

"Mrs. Silvers loved my chili that I entered into the cook-off so much that she thinks I should send the recipe to this."

"Are you going to?" Hannah asked me.

"Maybe, but I can only think of one thing right now—the Book. Did you guys come up with any ideas to get it back?"

Darbie held up a lanyard from the chili festival with a red poker chip duct-taped to it and grimaced.

"What's that?" I asked.

"A medallion. We'll hypnotize Charlotte, and she'll have no choice but to lead us right to the Book."

"It's a poker chip," Hannah said. "And we don't know anything about hypnosis."

"No," I said. "But I bet we know someone who does."

"Señora Perez?" Hannah asked.

We'd learned that Señora Perez, owner of the local Mexican cooking store, La Cocina, was one of the three original authors of the Book. Ever since we found out about the book, she had been sort of our unofficial "potion advisor." La Cocina was also the only place that stocked the special ingredients we need—Señora P always made sure she had what we needed.

Charlotte called to us from the back of the bus. "What's all that whispering, girls? Talking about secret recipes? Oh, do you have potion problems?"

Misty, Charlotte's sidekick, high-fived Charlotte and said, "Good one!"

We ignored them. It wasn't easy, but we did it so often, we'd gotten good at it.

"Let's go see Señora super speedy," Darbie said.

Hannah and I nodded.

"We'll run over right after soccer practice," I said.

"Unless we're frogs by then," Darbie said. "In which case we'll hop."

4

Just Add Facial Warts

I knew something was wrong the moment I sat down in Family and Consumer Sciences class, or F&CS, which is what we used to call Home Ec. There was no recipe. Mr. Douglass ALWAYS sets out a recipe in the kitchen areas so we can get started right away.

Darbie was a little late: messy hair, mismatched outfit. Pretty normal for Darbie. She took one look at me and said, "Kell, you look like someone just Rollerbladed over your favorite sandwich. Ha! Remember the time I did that and you got so mad? Your face was all, like, *blahh*!" She made a silly face.

I didn't answer her, even though I remembered the time.

"'Member?" she asked again.

"There's no recipe," I said.

Hannah, wearing a trendy new top that I wanted to borrow immediately, returned from taking an exploratory lap around the F&CS classroom. It wasn't a classroom, exactly. It consisted of six separate kitchen areas—a counter with space to chop, a sink, a stove on top of an oven, a microwave, and a bowl with some random ingredients. Our bowl had an avocado, a banana, an apple, and a bunch of carrots with green stems still attached. There was a seventh area in the front of the room where Mr. Douglass taught and demonstrated.

"I checked with everyone," she said. "They don't know what's going on. No one has recipes."

"What do you think's happening?" I asked.

Darbie shrugged. "I dunno. I was still trying to remember what kind of sandwich it was."

Hannah brushed her bangs out of her face. "Should I ask what she's talking about?"

"Probably not." I knew rehashing the Rollerblading-over-the-sandwich thing would annoy Hannah.

At that moment I overheard Charlotte in kitchen area number two saying, "He probably got fired."

I was about to throw an overripe avocado at her when Mr. Douglass dragged himself into the classroom.

He clapped twice, like he always does to get the class's attention. Usually his claps are loud and filled with enthusiasm for what he's about to tell us, but today they were sad, slow, unexcited claps.

He sighed loudly.

We waited for him to speak.

"I have," he started, "some very bad news. About as bad as news can get." He sighed again. "I have just come from a school board budget meeting, where we discussed . . ." He closed his eyes, lowered his head, and rolled his hands out for us to finish his sentence.

"The budget?" we chanted together.

"Duh," said Charlotte, twirling one of her perfect blond curls around her index finger.

"That's right. As it does every year, the district discusses budget cuts. The board has decided that to meet its budget, it will eliminate our Family and Consumer Sciences program, which they said was . . ." He dabbed his eyes with a handkerchief that was folded like a flower and tucked into the front pocket of his shirt. "Obsolete."

Obsolete? Obsolete?!

Hands popped up.

Whispering started.

"I said it before, and I'll say it again," he continued. "Cooking is an art. We need to use these tangles of emotions to improve our craft. Your assignment for today is to improvise. Use the ingredients in the pantry and fridge to make the saddest dish—dinner or dessert—that you can. Out of the depths of sadness and despair blooms the . . . the . . ." He buried his nose in his hanky and left the room without telling us what blooms.

"This is terrible," I said.

"As bummerino as a stinkfest convention," Darbie said.

I overheard Charlotte say, "Who cares?"

I grabbed a frying pan and headed toward kitchen area two, but Hannah stopped me. "Don't start anything," she said. "Let's just cook. What's the saddest thing you can make?"

"I don't know. Cooking makes me happy, not sad."

"How about onions?" asked Darbie. "They make me cry. We can add broccoli to it. There isn't anything more depressing than a green vegetable. How about brussels sprouts? Even the name sounds depressing, like someone sprouted fingerlike tentacles all over her body."

"What can you do with that, Kell?" Hannah asked.

"I guess we could caramelize the onions and shred the sprouts. Maybe add some pine nuts."

"And yesterday's coffee grounds, and stinky cheese," suggested Darbie.

Hannah said, "We're going for sad, not food poisoning."

"You'd be sad if you were stinkier than all the other cheeses."

Darbie had a point.

"We could add Gorgonzola," I said. "It's both stinky and tasty. And Mr. Douglass always has some."

"That sounds downright dismal," Darbie said. "I'd be unhappy if I were called Gorgonzola."

Hannah agreed. "I'm mopey just thinking about it."

"Then maybe we should toss in just a few bloodred cranberries to liven it up," I suggested. "We don't want anyone getting too depressed."

"Sounds like a plan." Hannah went to the front of the F&CS room to shop around for the items that we needed. Stinky cheeses and pine nuts weren't popular items, probably because no one knew how to cook with them, so they were easy to find. But the onions were in high demand.

Hannah called Darbie for assistance. When Darbie marched with purpose toward the onion battle, the girl holding the last onion dropped it and walked away. No one wanted to duel with Darbie.

"Good work, team," I said when they returned with our goods. "I have some sea salt in my backpack. That will be good with this."

"Because we all carry around seasoned salt," Hannah said.

"Oh, it's not seasoned," I said.

"My mistake," Hannah said. "Then it's totally normal."

While I was rooting around in my bag, I saw the flyer Mrs. Silvers had given me about the Felice Foudini Recipe Challenge. I set it on our kitchen counter with the sea salt.

While I peeled the onion, Hannah examined the application. "Did you read this, Kell?"

"Just the headline."

Hannah said, "The prize is ten big ones."

"Ten bucks?" Darbie asked. "Big whoop."

"Ten *thousand* bucks!" Hannah corrected. "That money could help the F and CS Program. How perfect would that be? 'The cooking nut that saves her favorite class.'"

Darbie said, "That would be like me saving . . . saving . . . Hmm, I guess it's not like me at all, because I don't like classes."

"If anyone can win, we can." Then Darbie added, "With the Book, we can't lose."

Hannah said, "Any bad-luck price would be worth ten thousand dollars."

"Totally," Darbie said. "Unless it involves boogers or facial warts or snakes. Actually, I could probably handle facial warts, because then I could wear a mask, which, frankly, I would enjoy. So I guess facial warts would be okay. Man, I hope it's facial warts."

"Two problems," I said. "Public enemy number one has the Book. And second, Felice Foudini won't have the right spices to make a potion."

"Well, there goes the ranch . . . *and* the mask," Darbie said. "Thanks a lot. I was just getting excited."

"You can win without the Book," Hannah asked.

"She'll get entries from all over the country," I said. "Probably from chefs with a lot more experience than me."

"So it'll need to be a mega-awesome recipe," Darbie said. "If only there was a way that we could tell which of your recipes was the all-time best."

"Maybe there is," Hannah said. "Can you guys handle things here?"

"We sure can," Darbie assured her, and she took off on some type of mission.

I've known Darbie a long time. She meant that *I* could handle the cooking, and *she* could handle watching me.

Mr. Douglass had returned, and Hannah asked him for the hall pass, which he handed over, leaving one hand covering his face.

I chopped the onion and dropped it in a pan of hot olive oil the way I'd seen Felice Foudini do on her show a thousand times. It sizzled, and in a second the fragrance of caramelizing onions drifted into the hallway, luring in the only boy in F&CS. Mr. Douglass didn't even notice how late he was.

Frankie Rusamano bent down to smell. "What's going on in that pot, Kell?"

"We're making the saddest thing we can, because F and CS is going to be shut down because of budget cuts, which is sad," Darbie said. "But Kelly's going to win the ten-thousand-dollar prize from the Felice Foudini Recipe Challenge, so everything should be okay soon."

"Gotcha," Frankie said. "But this doesn't smell sad. It smells good. Can I have some?" He tried to steal a piece of onion, but Hannah wrested the fork away.

Hannah had a thing for Frankie, a crush kind of thing that she didn't admit. Meanwhile, I liked his fraternal twin Tony, but that was my secret.

I had given Tony Love Bug Juice (a love potion from the Book) a few weeks ago. I thought it was working, but it was hard to tell since he's quiet to begin with. I've been feeling guilty about potioning him into liking me, and I'm planning to give him a Moon Honey drop to undo it, but I haven't yet. But I will. But I'm afraid that then he won't like me anymore.

I sprinkled in brown sugar and handed Frankie the brussels sprouts. "Can you wash these?"

"I can try, Kell," he said, like he was honestly not sure if he'd succeed. "You know these are like little baby cabbages?" he asked as he rinsed them.

"I've noticed." I chopped the sprouts into shreds, added them to the onions and oil, tossed in some pine nuts, and added a dash of this and a dash of that. Then I let it simmer.

Hannah ran back into the F&CS room. "It's all set," she said.

"What is?" I asked.

"You're going to cook lunch for the whole seventh grade tomorrow. They'll vote on which dish is the best, and that's the recipe we'll submit to the challenge. I cleared it."

"How did you clear that so fast? Don't important people need to know and fill out forms and stuff?" I asked.

"Of course. I spoke to the principal, who Skyped with the head of the school board. They filled out the online forms, which were e-mailed to our parents to sign and provide insurance info blah-blah-blah, which they did right away—our moms have gotten so good at doing those things on their phones—and, presto! We can cook in the caf."

"How am I going to cook lunch for all those people?"

"You've gone through the slots of the spatula this time, Hannah-Spammy-Miami," said Darbie. Ever since we were little, Darbie has added a little spice to Hannah's name. Hannah doesn't like it.

"We're gonna help you," Hannah said to me.

I looked at them. "That doesn't make me feel better."

"Me and Tony'll help too," Frankie said.

"You sure will," Hannah said. "Your mom signed the forms too."

Mr. Douglass's cell phone rang, and, after a loud sigh, he answered. As he listened, his face brightened around his puffy redness, and he rushed over to us. "That call was about your excellent idea, Kelly and Company. I agreed to chaperone." He clasped his hands together. "I feel so much better. Now I just have to do something about these puffy eyes."

"Try cucumbers," Frankie suggested.

We all looked at him with shock that he would know to suggest this.

"It's what my mom does," he explained.

"Brilliant idea, Franklin." Mr. Douglass made his way to the fridge to tend to his skin.

Hannah said, "Now you have enough people. All you need to do is pick the recipes."

"What are your three most amazing specialties?" asked Darbie.

"Only three?"

"The velvety red-carpet cake," Frankie said.

"Obvs," Darbie and Hannah agreed.

"How about that Slowpoke Cooker Fettuccine?" Darbie asked. "I love that one."

"Oh, I know," Hannah said. "The Veggie Enchi-la-di-das. It adds the healthy angle. Felice Foudini would love that."

"Enchi-la-di-das," Darbie sang, and added a dance. "Enchi-la-di-das."

Mr. Douglass called back to us, "LLJ said she needs your shopping list double ASAP."

LLJ was Lunch Lady Julie. We were afraid of her on account of her muscles and tats and the fact that she always looked really mean.

"Um," Darbie said. "How about if we give you the list to give to her?"

"You're going to lunch right after this. Just give it to her then."

Frankie said, "You're afraid of her, aren't you?"

"If you aren't, then you can give her the list," Hannah said.

"Fine. Give it to me," he said. "I'll make Tony do it."

5

Isla de Cedros

Coach Richards yelled through an orange cone as if it were a megaphone. "You're late! How can you be captain today if you're late, Darbie O'Brien? The captain is supposed to set an example."

Charlotte smirked, basking in the notion of Darbie falling short of the high expectations of captain of the Alfred Nobel School girls' soccer team, the ANtS.

"Got it, Coach." Darbie directed the team, "Let's take a warm-up lap."

"Five!" Coach yelled.

"Five?" Darbie asked him. "Coach, on behalf of the team, I think that's a little more than a warm-up."

He pulled Darbie aside, but I was close enough to hear. "If it's too much for you—" His phone buzzed with a text, and he glanced down to look at it.

"It's not too much. I swear. I got this." Then she pointed to his phone. "And I figure you've got *that under control*."

"Don't read other people's texts," he said. "But, yeah, I got that."

"Okay, team," Darbie announced. "Let's do a five-lap warm-up. Come on. It'll be fun," she encouraged. "We can sing."

Another round of groans indicated that no one was interested in singing while they ran.

"What's his deal today?" I asked.

Darbie said, "The Groundhogs' coach, Coach Madden, sent him a text talking smack about our game against them. I saw it. It said, 'Groundhogs crush ants.'"

"That kind of thing just isn't necessary," Hannah said. "Does their rivalry have to be so cutthroat? What's wrong with just regular old friendly competition?"

I said, "It's always been that way with Groundhogs and ANtS."

"Pick up the pace, girls! Let's HUSTLE!" he yelled.

When the five laps were done, we ran up and down the bleachers, moved huge logs from one side of the field to the other, lunged around the parking lot with rocks in our hands, and ended with sit-ups. Two hundred! No one even touched a ball.

"Hey, great job, captain," Charlotte said to Darbie. "I don't think the team has ever liked me as much as they do right now, so thanks for that."

After Charlotte walked away, Darbie asked us, "What was I supposed to do?"

"I don't know," I said. "Maybe we need to find a way for Coach Richards and Coach Madden to bury the hatchet."

"Do we have a potion for that?" Hannah asked. For Hannah to suggest a potion was a big deal, because it wasn't until recently that she believed they had special powers. She was a real skeptic, but since we learned the story of the Book, she's come around.

"We can look," I said. "No Return could be as bad as that workout."

We lay on the grass and chugged water. "Do you think Sam has an ice cream that will make us feel better?" Hannah asked.

"I've never met an ice cream that could make feel me worse," Darbie said. "So it would be irresponsible for us not to try it."

"Totally," I agreed. "Let's go see Sam and Señora P to ask her about hypnosis and buy some Cedronian spices. We have a serious shortage."

The magical ingredients came from the *Isla de Cedros* in Mexico, where Señora P is from. Whenever she goes back, she's able to bring us everything we need from her local healer and shaman, who sources those spices.

After practice, we hobbled down Marsh Road toward the stores. "Do you think she'll be mad that we lost it?" I asked.

"Lost is a strong word," Darbie said. "It was donated, which is really a nice thing, so how can she be mad about charity? And"—she rubbed her calves—"will one of you carry me?"

"We're almost there." Hannah enticed her. "There's ice cream."

"Those are the magic words," Darbie said, and pressed onward.

It was in our sights. La Cocina's windows were dark, but that was nothing new. It was always dimly lit, dusty, and downright spooky. Truthfully, I didn't love going in there. I was always afraid that Señora P's crow would fly into my hair and make a home there, but this was the only place we could get the special ingredients.

"Is that a sign in the window?" Hannah asked.

Darbie said, "I can only see fuzzy little spots before my eyes. I'm dehydrated. I'm sure of it. Ice cream is the only thing that will help my condition. I need the biggest Super Swirley Sam can make. He might have to put it in a bucket, because a regular cup won't hold the puppy I need to rehydrate."

Hannah ignored Darbie. (She does that a lot.) "It's definitely a sign."

We got close enough to read it.

"Oh no," I said.

6

Gone to Mexico

Gone to Mexico?" Darbie asked. "How can Señora just leave town when we need her?"

"She could've told us," Hannah said. "And maybe given us a plan for a potion emergency, because she knows how deep we are in recipe experimentation."

"Maybe she's getting more ingredients," I said.

"That woman should have a light, like the Bat-Signal, that we could shine into the sky, and she could see it in Mexico and know we were in trouble."

"Or," Hannah suggested, "a cell phone."

Señora P wasn't the type to have either.

"Let's get Swirleys and figure out our next step," I said.

We limped into Sam's iScream, home of the Super Swirley, which is the most amazing ice cream concoction on the East Coast, and possibly the world. We come here so much that we don't even have to tell Sam our order anymore: I get Black and White, Darbie gets Rocket Launching Rainbow, and Hannah gets Bowl Me Over Chocolate Brownie.

"If we can figure out the other two authors of the Book, we can ask one of them for help," I suggested, then took the first amazing sip.

"Good idea," Hannah said. "What do we know about them?"

"According to Señora P, she and two other girls wrote the Book the summer when she was about twelve years old," I started.

"She said they went to the pool together, remember?" Hannah asked.

"So we can hypotenuse that the other two are about her same age," Darbie said.

"'Hypothesize,'" Hannah corrected.

"Sure. If you want to," Darbie said, clearly not knowing "hypotenuse" or "hypothesize."

"We know their initials," I said. After studying the Book,

we figured out that some of the recipes had initials, like they'd been signed by the girl who created it. The three sets of initials were IP (we knew that's Ida Perez), RS, and KE. We didn't know who RS or KE were, and Señora P wouldn't tell us.

Darbie asked, "Why do you think Señora P was so secretive when we asked her about those other two names?"

"Probably because things didn't end well," I said.

Hannah picked up the story. "She said they'd made a potion with effects that they couldn't undo, so they sacrificed the biggest thing they could think of—they stopped cooking. That's when they pasted their recipes into the old encyclopedia to hide them. Then they stopped hanging out together. And, slowly, things returned to normal."

I added, "Creating the Book brought them together for the best summer of their lives, and the Book tore them apart."

"It's a sad story," Darbie said. "Can you change the ending? I'll sleep better if it's a happy ending."

Hannah said, "We can't change history."

"If only we could go back to that summer and tell them not to do that one potion," Darbie said.

"Or, if we could go back, we could see who her friends were," I said. "But, unless you have a time machine, I don't think we're gonna be able to do that."

"Then we'd better get started," Darbie said.

"With what?" Hannah asked.

"The time machine."

Hannah sighed, frustrated.

I said, "With the missing Book, impending doom of F and CS, and a coach situation, maybe we can save time travel for another day."

"Fine," Darbie said. "Next week, though, for sure."

Just then our phones chirped with a text. It was Charlotte.

She had sent us a selfie. And she was holding the Book.

7

We're Back, Baby!

Coach Richards, who was also our science teacher, was writing on the board when we arrived at first period the next day. This was the only class we had to go to this morning, because we were making lunch for seventy-five kids. I thought maybe Coach was back to his old self until he kept writing and writing and writing, pressing down real hard on the chalk.

Finally, once the whole board was full, he took the last tiny nub of chalk and tossed it into the trash can. He didn't speak; he just slumped over his carrot juice and pointed to the first two words, which were all in caps:

GENEALOGY PROJECT. Under it were detailed instructions. We had to write a paper about our family history and give an oral report, due Monday. It would count for half of our grade.

There was a knock at the door, and in walked Tony Rusamano with two things: a thick, padded yellow envelope and a haircut. I was able to see his eyes clearly, and they looked straight at one person in the class—me.

I smiled at the attention, then stared at the floor. I really liked that Tony was noticing me, but it was immediately followed by a pang of guilt that I'd potioned him into doing it.

Tony handed the envelope to Coach Richards, who didn't seem to notice it was there, so Tony delivered it directly to the recipient—me.

I resisted the urge to turn my head and watch him leave the classroom. Once everyone was working on their projects again, I opened it and peeked inside. I didn't have to remove the contents because I knew from a quick glance what it was—just your everyday boring old *World Book Encyclopedia, Volume T.*

There was a loose piece of paper with it. It said, *From KE.*

I didn't know who the second author was, but apparently she knew me. I passed the note to Hannah, who then shared it with Darbie, who exclaimed, "We're back, baby!"

Ordinarily Charlotte would've made an announcement

and spilled the beans about the Book to everyone. Except that the last time she had done that—she'd said something like "Kelly Quinn has a book of magic potions"—no one had believed her, and she was a laughingstock. So we'd narrowly escaped public humiliation.

Could we be that lucky twice?

Everyone looked up, including Charlotte, who quickly sized up the situation: Book-size envelope and our smiling faces. She knew we had it.

8

Allow Me to Introduce LLJ

Mr. Douglass's iPod was plugged into a speaker and blasted some pop songs for the whole cafeteria kitchen to hear.

"The girls are here!" he said when we entered.

Frankie and Tony walked in behind us. "So are we."

A grunt that could've been "Me too" came from near the walk-in freezer. It was LLJ. Based on her frosty eyelashes, I thought she might've slept in there last night.

I had a Moon Honey drop—the antidote for any potion—in my pocket for Tony. I didn't want to give it to him, because I liked the attention I was getting from him, but I knew that I had to because I couldn't deal with the guilt. Usually we think of all kinds of clever ways to give people a Moon Honey drop without them knowing, but I didn't think I needed to go to those extremes with Tony.

I took out two candies. "Want one?"

He took it and popped it right into his mouth. I pretended to do the same, but I saved it. Our supply was limited, and with La Cocina closed, I didn't know when we were going to be able to restock. I wondered, would he like me for real? I crossed my fingers, even though I didn't think those good-luck things worked.

"We have three hours till lunch. I've made a schedule," Hannah said. "We need to get the slow cookers going first."

"How many do we have?" I asked.

LLJ disappeared into a walk-in pantry and returned bear-hugging large electric pots. "Five," she said with a low, gruff, scratchy voice.

"Super," I said. Everyone took a pot, and I directed them through the recipe for Slowpoke Cooker Fettuccine. Tony needed some extra help, so I showed him how to level off a teaspoon of black pepper. As I measured, his hand touched mine. There was a little spark or a tingle or a shiver, I think. Wasn't there? Maybe it was just me.

Once the cookers were going, Hannah said, "Next up is cake."

We made the batter and baked twelve velvety red-carpet cakes. While they baked, we prepped large pans of Veggie Enchi-la-di-das, which prompted Darbie to show everyone her dance.

Hannah showed us the voting process she'd designed. She'd labeled shoe boxes—one for each dish. Every kid would get a taste of all four dishes and one ticket. They'd drop their ticket into the box for the dish they liked best. Simple.

When the cakes were cool enough, I demonstrated how everyone should ice the cakes, and set them to work on the others. I checked their work and saw LLJ bent over the cake I'd just finished.

What was she doing?

"Hey!" I called to her.

She stepped away, and I saw that she'd added red food coloring to the icing and, using a decorating bag with a metal tip, had made a dainty lattice pattern over top of the white icing. It was really pretty, and looked like Mrs. Silvers's lace doilies.

"I meant to say, *Hey that looks nice*," I backtracked.

"Wow," Darbie whispered to me. "Do you think she learned that in prison?" Darbie isn't a good whisperer.

LLJ asked, "Why does everyone assume I've been to prison?"

Never one to hold back, Darbie explained. "Well, that's the legend. When you leave here, you go check in with your parole officer."

She frowned. "That's what everyone thinks?"

Darbie nodded. "Yeah. You kinda have a vibe that's . . . well . . . that's scary."

I shoved a chunk of cake that had broken off the side of the pan into her mouth to shush her.

"I don't know where that vibe is coming from," LLJ said as she twisted her thick neck from left to right, making an awful cracking sound.

"So you're not out on parole?" Frankie asked. "Isn't this job part of your community service?"

"No. I'm a chef, so I cook here."

"So the legend is *wrong*." Darbie was dumbfounded with the concept of a legend, a.k.a. rumor, being wrong.

"'Fraid so. When I leave here, I meet my bowling team on Mondays and Wednesdays, and on Thursdays I tap-dance." She clicked her toes and heels and sang, "En-chi-la-di-das!"

Darbie whispered to Hannah, too loudly again, "She stole my song."

Hannah nudged her. "Shh."

"The icing looks really nice," I said. "Thanks."

"You're welcome." To Darbie, she said, "You're not."

When LLJ turned to finish the lattice, Darbie stuck out her tongue.

My phone chirped with a text. "My mom is here with the chili I made last night. She's backing up the minivan by the kitchen door right now."

"We'll get it," Frankie said, and he and Tony went to the kitchen doors to get the chili. Mom had kept it warm all morning, so it was all ready to go.

Mr. Douglass clapped his hands and stood on an overturned milk crate. "I just want to say thank you." He sniffed back tears of joy. "I don't think there has ever been a group of students this dedicated to the culinary arts." He probably would've said more, but luckily, he was too broken up to continue.

LLJ said, "Okay. No more mushy gushy. On with the show. People will be coming in soon."

Our classmates started piling into the cafeteria, jostling for a place in line. A few of the usual teachers who did lunch duty were there too.

Everyone left the line with four small plates on their tray with our dishes. Hannah gave out tickets, while my new friend LLJ watched over the boxes to prevent any monkey business.

Mrs. Eagle, the school librarian known for her ultrasonic hearing—seriously, she could hear things that happened in rooms she wasn't even in—came bustling over. She pretty much knew everything that happened at Alfred Nobel.

"Great job, everyone." She videotaped the whole event for the school website.

Charlotte Barney sidled up to the cafeteria line and grabbed a bottle of water. Tony handed her a bowl of fettuccine. "No thank you, Tony Rusamano," she said. "When I heard about this . . . this . . . *nonsense*, I packed my own lunch today. I don't trust this crew one bit. I know exactly what they're up to—"

Coach interrupted, "You're holding up the line, Barney. If you don't want any, just move along so the rest of us can get ours."

Charlotte harrumphed and did as Coach said.

Coach Richards took two bowls of fettuccine and two plates of enchiladas. "I'm taking hers." I sensed Coach, who was usually all about celery and apples, had an extra big appetite from watching us train so hard.

When lunch was over, Darbie, Hannah, the Rusamanos, and I sat at a cafeteria table and counted the votes. I sat next to Tony looking for any sign or spark. There was none.

"It's close," Hannah said. "But Slowpoke Cooker Fettuccine won!"

Darbie called to Mr. Douglass, who'd started cleaning up the cafeteria, "Did you hear that? Fettuccine took the gold!"

"Oh, gold is one of my favorite colors!"

LLJ heaved up a tub of dirty dishes and rested it on her

head. "I like me some periwinkle myself. Good color. Hey, how about you boys bring those pots into the kitchen and start 'em soaking?"

"You got it, LLJ," Frankie said. He nudged Tony in the arm, pushing him right into me. "Come on, slugger."

The boys headed toward the kitchen while Darbie and Hannah cleaned up the tickets and shoe boxes. I took a nibble of my plate of fettuccine. It was good, but would it be good enough?

"What's wrong, Kell?" Hannah asked.

"I can do better," I said. "This sauce. It needs to be even better to win. Different. Felice Foudini is going to get recipes from all over the country. Mine needs to really stand out."

"How are you going to make it different?" she asked. "New and exciting?"

"I'm not gonna jump on something new and trendy, anyone can do that. I think I need something old . . . something tried-and-true that I can reinvent."

"There were more cookbooks in your attic, you know," Darbie said. "I saw them when we were cleaning up there, but I didn't touch them, because they remind me of homework."

"I'll scour through them tonight," I said. "I'll find something that everyone has forgotten about."

"Look what's coming," I mumbled when I saw Charlotte

Barney enter the caf. Then I eyed my backpack, in which sat the Book.

"Ugh!" Darbie said loud enough to be rude.

"I don't like you, either, Darbie O'Brien," Charlotte said. "I want you to know that I've been watching you three. And I know everything. *Everything.*"

We waited for the threat that inevitably had to follow a statement like that. Charlotte had to want something. And did she ever.

New Members to the Secret Cooking Club?

Wearing yellow rubber gloves, we scrubbed the pots in the cafeteria's colossal sinks.

I said to Mr. Douglass, "We can finish things here." By "we" I meant me, Darb, and Hannah. Charlotte went back to class after dropping the bomb that she wanted to be in the secret cooking club, or else. . . . And the boys were sweeping and wiping tables in the eating area of the cafeteria.

"Really? You mean it? Because I would give anything to elevate my feet and relax with a eucalyptus tea."

"You totally should," I said. "Thanks so much for all your help today."

"You are very welcome." Mr. Douglass filled a mug with hot water and asked LLJ, "Care to join me?"

"Eucalyptus? Heck yeah. I love that junk. Relaxes me."

"And thanks to you, too, LLJ," I added.

"Yeah, thanks," Darbie and Hannah chimed in.

Darbie added, "Sorry I thought you'd been a criminal."

LLJ said, "It's okay."

When they'd gone, Darbie asked, "Why did you get rid of those extra cleaning hands? This is going to take us forever."

"Because we have work to do. About Charlotte. And we can't have them around while we search the Book for an idea."

"What about *them*?" Hannah indicated the boys, who were sorting the steaming-hot silverware as it came out of the dishwasher.

Darbie asked, "Are we gonna let them in it—the club? You know, initiate them? I'm talking the handshake, knock, password, the whole enchi-la-di-da?"

"Maybe we can just let them hang out without all the fixin's." I added, "That can be for just us, as the founders."

"I like it," Darbie said. "They can be like our interns and do all the boring work."

"Good plan. Let's stick a pin in it and invite them when the time is right," I said.

"Ahem." We glanced over and saw Ralph French, a sixth grader who had walked in while we were talking.

Darbie got right in his face and asked him, "How much did you hear?"

Ralphie's knees quaked. "Something about interns. That's all. I swear."

Darbie pointed to the bag he was carrying. "What's that?"

"Dunno. I was just asked to deliver it."

Darbie took it. "You were never here. You never saw us," she said to him. "Now go away." Ralph took off.

"Was that totally necessary?" Hannah asked. "He nearly peed."

"We need to be careful," Darbie said, and opened the bag. "Looks like a little bottle of perfume, maybe." She pulled the cork out of a small, blue-tinted bottle and dabbed it behind her ear. "Ew. Sticky." She licked her finger. "But sweet."

I took the bottle and read the label. "Cedronian agave," I said. "I can add this to our dwindling stock of ingredients. With La Cocina closed, we don't have much to work with to hex Charlotte."

"What should we do?" Darbie asked.

"I don't know," I said. "I have to comb through the Book, but we need her to forget what she knows and about the evidence she has, or else we'll have to give her what she wants—to be in the club."

"I don't know why she would even want that," Hannah said.

"Because she knows we would hate it, and she lives to make us miserable," I said.

"Kell, for the official record, let me say this: The only way Charlotte Barney can join this club is over my dead body," Darbie said.

"Dead body?" Frankie asked as he and Tony walked over.

"Sorry, you don't have security clearance to know about that," Darbie said. "Maybe when you're initiated."

It wasn't uncommon for Frankie and Tony to have no idea what Darbie was talking about, so the bizarre answer didn't faze them. "Our work here is done," Frankie said. "We're gonna hang out in LLJ's favorite spot in the fridge and eat cheese sticks so that we don't have to go to geometry."

"You are? That sounds like fun." Darbie was clearly looking for an invitation that didn't come.

When the walk-in refrigerator door closed, I crinkled my brows and thought carefully.

"What's wrong, Kell?" Hannah asked.

"Señora P is in Mexico and couldn't have sent this," I said. "So if she didn't send that agave . . . who did?"

10

Memory Maker Potion
Part One

With the boys tucked away in the fridge, we were in the clear to study the Book for something that would, as Darbie said, "Fix Charlotte good."

"See this?" Hannah asked. "Dumplings of Doom."

"Doom is a little intimidating," I said.

Darbie said, "But let's remember it, in case things get dire."

Then I saw something exciting. "Look at this one." I pointed to Memory Maker. "It's a three-part recipe."

"We haven't had one of those before," Hannah said.

"Part one is Eraser Lollipops, and guess what ingredient it needs," Darbie said.

"Cedronian agave," I said.

"How coincidental is that?" Darbie asked.

"Too coincidental," Hannah said.

I summarized. "Someone's helping us."

Darbie said, "Guess whose initials are next to the lollipops."

"KE?" I asked.

"Yup," she said.

Hannah looked at the clock. "What are we waiting for? If we make it now, we can bring lollipops to soccer."

Darbie asked, "And hex the whole team?"

"No way," Hannah said. "We'll add the agave to just one."

I stirred the sticky agave solution with a toothpick. "Who's going to add it?" I asked. "I don't think I can afford a Return until I finish the Felice Foudini Recipe Challenge. One of you guys has to take one for the team."

Darbie and Hannah looked at each other.

"Not it!" Hannah said.

"Wait. I didn't know we were racing to Not It," Darbie said.

"We were," Hannah said. "It's a game that never turns off."

"Fine," Darbie said. "I'll do it. But the next one goes to an intern."

I patted her on the back. "Thanks, Darb. You know this is important."

Darbie sneered as she let the gooey drops of blue agave drip into one of the Eraser Lollipops. "I like the idea of potioning that bully."

"That's the attitude," I said.

The lollipops were finished just as the end-of-the-day bell rang. Hannah put the agave back in the paper bag and put it into her front pocket. "I'm gonna borrow this for a little something to help with the Coach Richards problem."

"There's a Coach Richards problem?" Frankie asked as he emerged from the fridge.

Tony rubbed his hands up and down his arms to warm up.

Darbie said, "The Groundhogs' coach is hounding him that they're going to beat us."

Hannah said, "The two have always been rivals, but it's reached a whole new level."

"Well, good luck with that," Frankie said, and headed out of the kitchen. "I'm going home to binge-watch season three of *Turd Wars*."

"See you later," Tony said through his chattering teeth. He was so cute when he was cold. "I'm going to my locker, then hang out and watch your game."

Once they were gone, I reminded Darbie, "Don't forget

you have a Return coming for the pops." Then to Hannah, I said, "And you will too, if you potion Coach. I'll draw good deeds for both of you as soon as I get home tonight, and maybe if you start on them pronto, the Return won't have much time to get you."

Good deeds came from a pretty box covered with tapestry that Señora P gave us. A deed ends a Return.

"Sounds like a plan, Stan," Darbie said. "Now let's give the pop to that schlop. By 'schlop,' I mean Charlotte."

"We totally understood that," I said.

Hannah pulled a ribbon out of her ponytail and tied it to one pop stick. "This one is for Charlotte. The others have regular sugar for everyone else."

"You're a genius, Hannah-Honolulu."

11
Kicking Some Groundhog Butt

We changed into our soccer uniforms. Darbie walked around the locker room handing out lollipops to everyone. "Here you go, fellow ANtS! Here are high-protein, vegan, energy pops to lead us to victory."

"So good for you," Hannah said, taking one herself and sucking on it. "Mmmmm."

"I want one." Misty popped one in her mouth. "Actually, I'll take two."

"Only one per customer," Darbie said.

I figured she wanted it for Charlotte but that Charlotte was too embarrassed to ask for it herself. I said, "Oh,

Darbie, can't you make an exception? She loves your pops. Take it as a compliment."

Darbie narrowed her eyes at Misty and said, "Just this once." Then she handed Misty the pop with the red ribbon.

Misty slid the ribbon off and kept it and gave the pop to Charlotte.

"Don't look at her," I said to Darbie and Hannah. "Just stand here and act like we don't care if Charlotte eats that pop or not. Keep pretending that we're talking."

Hannah said, "We are talking."

"Good thing," Darbie said, "because she would totally know if we weren't."

"I think we should walk away," I said. "Because then it totally won't look like we're watching her."

"Then how will we know if she eats it?" Darbie asks.

"When her memory is erased," I said. "Follow me. Don't make any sudden moves. Act casual."

We started walking away, until Darbie climbed to the top of the row of lockers.

"What are you doing?" I asked her. "What happened to casual?"

"I wanna see if she eats it." She slid down the top of the lockers on her belly for a better view. A second or two later she slid back and gave us two thumbs up.

"What are you doing, O'Brien?" Charlotte called up to Darbie. "You're going to get the whole team in trouble for goofing around in the lock—"

She stopped mid-sentence.

"Is she choking?" Misty asked.

"Charlotte," I called out. "Are you okay?"

Darbie said, "Blink once if you need the Hemlock maneuver."

"'Heimlich,'" I corrected her.

"Potato, pataaato. Who cares, Kell? She's choking."

"Is she?" Hannah asked. "Looks like she's breathing."

Charlotte didn't blink, rather she made eye contact with me and asked, "What are you staring at, Kelly Quinn?"

"Phew!" I said. "We thought you were choking."

"No." Charlotte looked around the locker room. "Where are we going?"

"To kick some Groundhog butt!" Misty said about the opposing team, the Glen Mills Groundhogs.

Darbie said, "You two should probably walk to the field without the rest of the team, like you're too good for us."

"You aren't as dumb as you look." Misty pointed at Darbie with her pop. "Come on, Charlotte."

Hannah held her two hands down low, palms up, and Darbie and I gave her a double high five.

Mission accomplished.

* * *

Our archrivals, the Glen Mills Groundhogs, got off their bus. I don't know how or when the rivalry started, but I knew what was going to keep it alive—their coach, Erin Madden.

Coach Madden was tough, fit, and pretty, and her team loved her. She looked at Coach Richards and made a motion of her foot stomping and squishing an ant.

Coach Richards saw, then turned his back and called to us, "Huddle up, ANtS." We crowded around him. "Here's the deal. We canNOT lose to this team. We're going to run faster, head harder, kick farther, and shoot more accurately. Am I clear?"

"Yes, sir," we all said

"Good," Coach said. "Hop on that field and score some points."

Charlotte hopped onto the field like she was jumping on a pretend pogo stick.

In a nutshell, the first half of the game was a disaster. The Groundhogs scored in the first few minutes, largely because Charlotte seemed to have forgotten the rules. After she picked up the ball for the third time, Coach benched her, giving Darbie a chance to play. Darbie didn't do too badly. Regardless, at the end of the first half, the ANtS were down by four.

Coach Richards yelled a lot from the sidelines.

When Hannah came out for a water break, she said to him, "Coach, I think your blood sugar is getting low. Here, you can have my apple."

"Don't you need it?"

"I have a banana and a pear."

"Thanks, Hernandez." *Crunch!* "Now get back out there. And put it in the goal."

"You got it," Hannah said.

Hannah actually managed to kick the ball into the goal, improving things, but we still lost by six.

Once all the Groundhogs had left, Coach Richard said, "Don't even think about heading to the locker room yet. We're running the hill."

Ugh!

As we sprinted up, I asked Hannah, "I thought you gave him the apple?"

"I did."

"Do you think you mis-measured?" Darbie asked. "You know capital *T* is tablespoon? Not everyone knows that."

Hannah gave Darbie a look. "There was no mis-measuring," she snapped.

"You used the agave?" I confirmed.

"Of course. And obviously it worked for Charlotte, so it can't be that."

"It's a mystery," Darbie said. Then she dropped to the ground at the top of the hill. "Come back and get me when you've solved it."

"We're not done," Coach yelled. "O'Brien! Keep moving!"

"Roger that, Coach."

And Darbie rolled down the hill. "I'm moving," she hollered.

She reached the bottom of the hill, landing right at Coach's feet. "I'm not in the mood, O'Brien." Then he announced, "We're done. Have a good night."

"No chance of that," Hannah said, waddling to my mom's minivan.

"Hi, Mrs. Q. I'm sorry to say that I literally cannot close the door. My brain is sending signals to my arm, but my arm isn't lifting up."

Mom closed the door, sealing us all in the minivan.

And that's when Darbie's Return decided to kick in, and it was bad luck for all of us.

12

Farts, an Invitation, and a Good Deed

W ho's farting?" Bud, my six-year-old, pain-in-the-neck brother, asked.

My mom cracked a window.

"Sorry, guys. I can't help it," Darbie said. "They were slipping out through the whole game. I'm glad it was windy."

It happened again.

"It's your Return," I said.

My mom dropped Darbie off first, thankfully. As she slid the van door shut, Darbie said, "Don't forget to text me about you know what."

I knew what. A deed.

I had just enough energy after a shower and dinner to hit the attic.

My legs had gotten stiff from sitting through dinner, so I teetered from side to side when I walked. I bumped into the hall table as I passed it, knocking the mail to the floor. One of the envelopes caught my eye as I was picking everything up. It was super fancy with gold-trim. Maybe it was a wedding invite?

It was addressed to only my mom and included her middle name: Becky Smythe Quinn. Samantha used to be her middle name, like me and my grandmother, but when she got married, she moved her maiden name to the middle, and Samantha got the boot. The return address was from her high school in Massachusetts. The back of the envelope said *Reunion!*

I set it back on the table. Even though we weren't in high school yet, it made me wonder about Hannah, Darbie, and me in twenty years. *Would we still be friends?* I hoped so.

As I went up to the attic, I kept thinking about losing touch with my friends like the authors of the Book. I couldn't imagine going a single day without talking to Hannah and Darbie.

Speaking of Darbie . . . I needed to send her a good

deed before I went to bed. Hannah wouldn't need one since Coach's apple didn't work. *Why hadn't it worked?*

Before we'd cleaned a few weeks ago, the attic had been jam-packed with stuff that used to be my grandmother's and some stuff that belonged to Mrs. Silvers back from when her basement had flooded. Now it was cleared out except for ten boxes neatly stacked in a corner. And it was less dusty and spiderwebby but still totally creepy. The ceiling was low, the lighting was bad, and it was stuffy.

I scanned the boxes that were left and found the one I was looking for: BOOKS. Inside I found several cookbooks. I flipped through them looking for some old-fashioned, secret pearls of cooking wisdom that had long been forgotten or disregarded by modern cooks.

Ah! *The American Cookbook.* It had a picture of a loaf of bread on the cover and had once been green, but was faded now. The binding was cracked from being opened and closed so many times, and there were grease drippings and food splashes on the pages—the signs of a well-used cookbook. This was exactly the type of thing I was looking for. I could find a golden vintage nugget in here.

I made my way out of the attic and brought my new find to bed.

Before snuggling in, I looked in the recipe box covered in tapestry and lined with satin and took out one of the little pouches it held. These were the good deeds that Señora Perez had given us to undo Returns.

I untied the drawstring of the tiny sack and read the paper that was inside.

The paper said: *Help someone with their homework.* Oh jeez, that was gonna be hard for Darbie, because she usually doesn't even do her own homework. I texted her a picture of the paper. And she replied right away, **Easy peasy lemon squeezey.**

I knew she was being sarcastic. **Maybe a little kid,** I texted back.

You always have the best ideas, KQ!

How's your butt problem? I asked.

My butt's fine, but I'm cold. My mom keeps sending me outside when I feel one coming. And that's most of the time.

13
The Thing About Reference Books

The next morning, Saturday, I was zooming out my door to meet the girls at the library to work on our genealogy projects when I smelled something . . . strange and unpleasant.

I peeked in the kitchen and saw Darbie sitting at the table with Buddy. They had a book opened on the table.

"How are you . . . um . . . feeling?" I asked her.

"It's getting better," she said. "Buddy let me help him with his science."

"Yeah," Buddy said. "And she showed me how to rip the most amazing farts."

"Yup," Darbie confirmed; then to Buddy she said, "Only, I'm all out of gas now. So I think it's time for me to go."

"Not me," he said. "I am always full of it." *Pfft! Pfft!*

He laughed at himself.

"Gross," I said. "Let's go, Darb."

"Sure thing. Do you think maybe we should light a candle or something?"

"Good idea."

On our way to the library, I stopped, hopped off my bike, and scooped the dog poop out of Mrs. Silvers's yard. I figured it was good karma, and you can't have enough good karma when you're messing with potions.

Darbie waited for me on her bike and looked around the yard. "I never noticed that Mrs. Silvers has a spice garden."

"Me either. I'm used to dashing in and out of here fast, because I was scared to death that she was going to put some kind of hex on me."

"And now look—you two are like pals-ies, and we're the ones hexing."

Since it was October, there wasn't much left in the garden, but the rows still had their little signs: BASIL, ROSEMARY, THYME.

"I hadn't pegged Mrs. Silvers as a cook," Darbie said. "I thought of her more as a Chef Boyardee lady."

I shrugged, disposed of the poop, and got back on my bike.

Hannah was waiting for us with her foot tapping and arms crossed. "You're late."

"Sorry," I said.

Darbie went on to explain. "There was science homework, farting, dog poop, and spices. It's a long story, but here we are on Wilmington Road at the public library, ready to write those papers!" She pretended to be excited.

"It's on Wilmington Road," Hannah repeated. "Do you have the Book with you, Kell?" she asked me.

I nodded. "I'm not leaving it alone anymore."

"Can I see it?"

I handed it to her. She flipped through the regular encyclopedia pages until she got to the handwritten recipe pages. She pointed to the letterhead they were written on. It was stationery for the Wilmington Public Library. "This says it's on Main Street. I wonder when it moved?"

"Who cares?" Darbie asked.

"I do," Hannah said. "That's why I said it."

We went inside and approached Mrs. Sullivan's desk. She'd been the librarian since I was a little girl and Mom brought me to story time.

"Did this building used to be on Main Street?" Hannah asked her.

"Well, the building has always been right here, but before expansions and renovations, the entrance used to face Main Street, so that was the mailing address. Now our front door and parking lot face Wilmington Road," she explained. Meanwhile Darbie helped herself to the Hershey's Kisses on her desk. "The public only sees the new sections of the library—the renovated parts. But there are hallways and rooms as old as this town, where we store books that are no longer in demand. I suppose we should get rid of them, but . . ."

Hannah pulled me aside and whispered to me while Darbie was still involved with Mrs. Sullivan's story about the storage of old books, card catalogues, and periodicals.

"The authors would have gotten their paper from the old library. I think we need to check out those hallways and see if we can find any clues about KE and RS. Maybe one of them can tell us why the apple didn't work for Coach Richards."

"Right," I agreed. "But how?"

Hannah looked at Mrs. Sullivan, who now was talking about the reference section and library cards. "She's just getting started. She looks like she's been dying to tell someone all about this stuff forever. And Darbie will be an interested listener as long as those Kisses last."

I nodded.

Mrs. Sullivan was saying, "That space could probably be cleaned up and used for other things."

"You know," Hannah said. "Darbie loves local history. She's sort of a buff. You know, the type who can't get enough of it?"

"Oh yes, I know the type." Mrs. Sullivan lifted her hand. "Guilty as charged."

"Then you two will have so much to talk about," I said. "But Darbie has blood sugar issues. Do you have more Kisses?"

"I love Kisses," Darbie said.

Mrs. Sullivan reached under her desk and poured a whole new bag into the bowl.

"Perfect," I said. "Hannah and I need to get started on this project—shame we can't listen too, but Darbie will tell us all about it later."

Mrs. Sullivan took the bowl and led Darbie to a table in the children's section, where the two sat down and continued their talk.

"I think we should go that way." Hannah pointed to a door with a sign on it that said NO ENTRANCE.

I followed her.

Inside the door was a stairway that went down.

There was no light switch, so we used the flashlight app on our phones and wandered through what felt like catacombs. We entered a room called REFERENCE AND COLLECTIBLES.

"It's cold down here. Let's hurry," I said.

There were shelves of books, atlases, and dictionaries. There was a shelf that looked like parallel bars, from which yellowed newspapers hung over poles, and another area where magazines dangled from clips. Then we located a large bookcase filled with encyclopedias from different years. When we found the *World Book Encyclopedia* from 1953, we looked at all the letters. Sure enough, *T* was missing.

"It's from here. Our Book was right on this shelf. So the authors either stole it or checked it out," Hannah said. "They don't strike me as thieves. If they checked it out, there would be a record of it, and we'll know who they are."

"They wouldn't keep records that old," I said.

"Oh really?" Hannah said, pointing to a file cabinet that was labeled RECORDS.

We opened the metal drawer and started combing through the files, when we heard a sound.

Ping!

We froze.

Then there was the sound of something rolling on the ground.

Like a marble.

We looked down and saw the object.

Not a marble.

An orange M&M.

"Darbie?" I whispered.

"Where are you? I can hardly see," she said.

"In here."

She found us. "Thank God. Mrs. Sullivan ran out of Kisses, so she gave me a dollar to buy M&M's from the vending machine. How much longer are you going to be? I don't know how much longer I can take local history. She's past the Revolutionary War and moving on to Delaware's activity in the Underground Railroad. Did you know that it wasn't a railroad at all?"

"Most people know that." Hannah blew her bangs out of her face.

I asked. "Where's Mrs. Sullivan?"

"Waiting for me. She wants to tell me about gunpowder, Teflon, and Kevlar. Did you know all those things have roots in Delaware, Madam Smarty Pants?" she asked Hannah.

"Actually, no," Hannah said. "Go and listen carefully so you can tell me about it."

Darbie popped M&M's into her mouth. "So, what's going on here?"

We filled her in on what we'd discovered so far. "We need to see who checked the encyclopedia out," I said.

Darbie said, "That won't work."

"And why not?" Hannah asked.

"The thing about reference books is that you can't

check them out," Darbie said. "*Everybody* knows that."

Touché!

Darbie didn't leave it there. For good measure, she just had to toss in, "Want some lotion to smear on that burn?"

"It's *ointment*," Hannah said. "People put ointment on burns."

14

Fried Bat Wings

We joined Darbie to learn about the local invention of Kevlar. Once all the Kisses and M&M's were gone, we gracefully excused ourselves to work on our projects. We were behind schedule—Hannah always made a schedule for us. To make up for lost time, we agreed to sit in different sections of the library and not talk to each other for two hours, so that we could get it done, which was lonely, but it worked.

When we were all done, we sat outside on the grass, among a display of pumpkins and scarecrows, and we each did one practice run-through of our oral reports.

Just as Hannah was finishing, a Rusamano Landscaping truck pulled up. Frankie and Tony hopped out of the back, and the truck took off.

"Hey hey, what up, girl friends o' mine?" Frankie called. "Guess what we've got." He held up a white box.

Darbie gasped. "It isn't," she said. "Don't you dare joke about that, Frankie and Tony Rusamano. Just don't."

"No joke," Frankie said.

"Mom just finished 'em," Tony added.

He opened the box. Inside were three of Mrs. R's amazing homemade cannoli.

Darbie and Hannah each took one, and Tony handed one to me.

"Thanks," I said. I looked right into his blue eyes with long lashes. "I like your haircut, by the way."

He shrugged off the compliment.

"Is your submission for the double-F RC ready?" Frankie asked.

"Yup. I just finished it a little while ago after I was done with this report. It only took a few minutes"

Hannah asked, "Did you find something amazing in your attic last night?"

"No. The attic finding let me down. Turns out that they weren't the best cooks. Actually, I got the idea this morning on the way here when we stopped at Mrs. Silvers's to scoop poop. She has an herb garden that included one lesser-known herb that I'd sort of forgotten about. These days everything is about cilantro and rosemary."

My friends nodded like they knew about spice trends, but I knew they were just humoring me. They didn't know rosemary from rose hips.

I added, "And she was all decorated for Halloween. We've been so busy, we can't forget that the best day of the year is right around the corner."

Frankie asked me, "So, are you gonna forget about fettuccine and fry bat wings or something?"

"Ew, gross. No," I said. "I'm sticking with the pasta, but adding the mystery spice and giving it a seasonal flare. How does Fettuccine Zombie Noodles in a cauldron sound?"

Hannah said, "That's the whole package, Kell. It will taste awesome, look great, and be fun!"

"Exactly." I slapped the Felice Foudini Recipe Challenge paper down on the grass to let them see my cauldron artwork and lay back in the grass to enjoy the sun.

Tony looked at the paper. "I think you have—what is it you girls say? A *problemo*?"

15

Planjo Banjo

on't say *problemo*," Darbie said. "We don't like *problemos*."

"What's the deal?" Frankie asked Tony.

"Um. Submissions are due today."

"Today!?" we girls yelled.

I said, "That's it. We're too late. There's no way it'll get there on time. We're going to lose F and CS, and Mr. Douglass will be out of a job."

"And LLJ will go back to prison," Darbie said. "She was just starting to grow on me."

"This won't affect *her* job," Hannah said.

"And she isn't really on parole or even any kind of prisoner," I added.

"Who are you going to believe? Her or an honest-to-goodness school legend?" asked Darbie.

Hannah blew her bangs out of her face.

"Maybe LLJ and Coach can drive the submission up to Felice Foudini's people in New York City on Monday. A personal delivery. You know, some of my mom's cannoli. No one can turn *that* down," Frankie said.

I said, "We're not going to bribe Felice Foudini. We're just going to forget this whole stupid thing!" I stormed away and left the paper on the grass.

Hannah and Darbie chased after me. "What about plan B?" Hannah asked.

"There's a plan B?" Darbie asked. "A planjo banjo?"

"We go back to what's been working for us," Hannah said. "The Secret Recipe Book."

"We're also not potioning Felice Foudini," I said.

"No. I wasn't thinking we'd potion her," Hannah said. "What's standing in the way of F and CS?"

"Ten thousand smackers," Darbie said.

"And the school board," I said.

"Bingo," Hannah said.

"Banjo," Darbie corrected.

"You want to potion the school board?" I asked.

"Maybe just a few of them," Hannah said. "For a while, until we find another way to get the money."

"I guess we could do that," I agreed. "But we're seriously low on Moon Honey drops, so there's a chance we won't be able to reverse the potions until Señora P gets back."

"And there's no guessing when that will be," Hannah said.

16
The Trophy Case

It was just like any other Monday, except for the addition of Halloween decorations at Alfred Nobel School.

"What are you gonna be?" Darbie asked us.

"Don't you think we're getting a little old for trick or treat?" Hannah asked.

"Bite your tongue right this minute, Hannah-Hiawatha-Haha. I overlook a lot of the things you say that make me feel dumb or immature, but I will not—I repeat—I will NOT let you make me feel bad about loving Halloween or talk me into skipping trick or treat." Darbie stopped and looked at Hannah very seriously. "Got it?"

I'd never heard Darbie talk like that to anyone before.

Hannah had a straight face. "Okay, Darb. Sorry. We can totally trick-or-treat."

Darbie smiled again, instantly. "I'm so glad that's behind us." Then she looked into the trophy case as we walked past it. "What a cute pic of a young Señora P and those other ladies. They don't look much older than us there."

"Picture?" I asked.

We passed that trophy case everyday on our way into school, but we'd never noticed the picture Darbie was referring to. It was among yearly photos of Chili Festival winners. Front and center, from 1959, was one of a young Señora Perez with two other women.

"The other two authors of the Book?" Hannah asked.

"Recognize her?" I pointed to one.

"Yup," Hannah said.

"I think I suddenly need to renew a library book," I said.

"Me too," Hannah said.

"Me too," Darbie said. "Ha! Just kidding. I don't take out any books that would need renewing. You should know that."

"Just come on," I said.

We walked into the library, and there she was, waiting for us.

KE.

17

The Summer of 1959

Mrs. Eagle, the school librarian with the rolling *r*'s and ultrasonic hearing, was waiting for us.

"I knew you were coming," she said. "Were" was like "werrre."

"How?" I asked.

"I know everything around here," Mrs. Eagle said. She pointed to her ears. "That's the problem with potions. If you don't take a Moon Honey drop, it doesn't reverse. I like it. I've known what you've been up to all along."

"And you're just telling us now?" Darbie asked. "You could have been helping us?"

"Some things you need to learn for yourself," she said.

"You got the Book back for us? You sent it to me in science class in the envelope?" I said.

Mrs. Eagle nodded.

"Why?" Hannah asked.

"You think that Charlotte Barney can handle it? I don't."

"And the Cedronian agave?" Hannah asked. "You sent Ralphie French to the cafeteria to give it to us, didn't you?"

She nodded.

Darbie had caught on. "You knew that Charlotte was going to expose us, and you wanted us to get her!"

"Not 'get her,' but I knew there was a lollipop recipe, because I wrote it myself . . . so, so many summers ago."

"Tell us about it," I said.

"And also tell us why the apple didn't work for Coach Richards," Hannah said.

"You have so many questions, and we don't have much time," Mrs. Eagle said. "The summer of 1959 was hot."

"All summers are hot," Darbie said.

"This was hotter than average. Look it up in *The Old Farmers' Almanac*. You will find it in the reference section."

"Speaking of reference sections," Hannah said, "we were at the public library recently—"

"Did you know they had a change of address?" Darbie chimed in as though she knew all about the library. "Mrs. Sullivan and I are friends, by the way. She lets me call her

'Sully,' so I'm practically part of the librarian community."

"Practically," Mrs. Eagle agreed with her. "Sit down. I will tell you what I can."

We sat a table in the computer section.

"I worked at the library that summer. Books were my best friends."

"Unpopular, huh?" Darbie asked.

"Darb!" I nudged her to tell her she was being rude.

"My only friends. Until, that is, a new girl came to town."

"Señora P," Hannah said.

"Yes. She worked at her parents' produce market and told me so much about herbs and spices, the types of things that I could not find in books."

"Like the *Isla de Cedros* and the shaman?" I asked.

"Exactly."

"One day another girl—I knew of her because she was very popular—overheard us and said there was no such thing as special spices. She was a lover of science, and she knew that a shaman couldn't change the chemical components of an herb."

"She reminds me of you," I said to Hannah.

"This other girl also loved to cook," Mrs. Eagle said.

"Now she reminds me of you, Kell," Hannah said.

"So we decided to team up and experiment. And that's what we did the whole summer. We used stationery that I got from the library, and we wrote it all down."

"But then things went bad?" Darbie asked, and then

she frowned. "Señora P told us about the boy."

Mrs. Eagle sat up very straight. "The boy. Oh, that boy." She looked like she was watching a flashback in her head. "He had been mean to us at the pool, so we hexed him, each of us adding a little bit of the ingredient so that we could equally share the Return. And the next day . . ."

"He was gone," I helped her finish the terrible memory, which we already knew from Señora P.

"Yes." A tear dripped from her eye. "The Return was the guilt we felt. We just wanted to teach him a bit of a lesson. We did countless good deeds to cancel the Return, but the guilt never faded. So instead, we made a sacrifice—"

"Like you killed something?"

"Dear me, no. We gave up something we loved. Cooking. And after a few days, he came back home. . . ."

"But he couldn't see," I said. The words seemed too painful for Mrs. Eagle to mutter.

"School started a few days later. We gave the boy Moon Honey every chance we could, and slowly he regained his eyesight. We vowed not to make any more recipes. And we hid them."

"You took *Volume T* from the library?" I asked.

She nodded. "The new set had arrived, so I ripped out the middle pages of an old volume and pasted in the stationery."

"It was a smart way to hide it," Hannah said.

Mrs. Eagle smiled. "It is not the only thing we hid."

18

Salem, Massachusetts

I stood in front of my science class. "I learned that my family was originally from Massachusetts. The oldest relative I could find was born in 1669, and her name was Rebecca Kelly Smythe. Rebecca continues to be a family name; my mom goes by Becky. Some Smythe traits are that we all have dark blond hair and a crooked tooth right here." I pointed to one of my canines. "Quinns are good at math, and Smythes love to cook. Thank you. The end."

Next was Charlotte's turn. "I don't remember much of my report. In fact, I can't even remember what I did this weekend. Is it lunchtime yet?"

"No playing around, Charlotte," Coach said. "This is a big part of your grade."

I whispered to Hannah and Darbie, "You know that I can't stand this girl, but this is painful to watch. We have to do something."

Darbie said, "I'm enjoying it."

Charlotte said, "I think we were circus people—" She patted her head and rubbed her stomach at the same time to prove that she had circus-performer genes.

Hannah said, "Fine. We'll help her. Darbie, make a distraction."

"My specialty," Darbie said, and presto! She launched into a fit of uncontrollable sneezes.

Totally made up, yet totally convincing.

Hannah smashed our last Moon Honey drop with her science book, and, while everyone was counting Darbie's tenth, eleventh, twelfth sneeze, Hannah blew the dust into Charlotte's face.

"Ugh. What the heck, Hannah Hernandez? Keep your dust away from me." Charlotte turned to Darbie and asked, "Are you quite done?"

Darbie sat down. "Yes. Thanks. I'm fine now."

Charlotte said, "The Barneys have had a significant place in history. General Barney crossed the Delaware River with George Washington, my great-great-aunt was one of the literary elite who sat at the Algonquin Round

Table, and my second cousin was advisor to President Ford." She continued, "The Barneys made their mark on Delaware as land developers. We are known for our beauty, brains, business acumen, natural sports abilities, and perfect blue eyes."

"Very nice, Charlotte," Coach Richards said. "If you're done, you can take your seat."

"There's one more thing I would like to report," she said. "Kelly Quinn has a magic book, and she's been putting spells on everyone for weeks. Darbie O'Brien and Hannah Hernandez have been helping her." She propped her hands on her hips, satisfied with herself, and stood in front of the silent, stunned classroom.

Frankie Rusamano made the first sound.

He laughed.

At first it was a snicker that he was trying to hold in, but it slipped out. Then it grew until it was loud and from the gut. Then Tony joined in, equally as hearty.

Soon the whole class was laughing at Charlotte.

"Good one," Frankie said.

"I am not joking around, Frankie. Our own Kelly Quinn is a *witch*!"

At that even Coach Richards laughed. "Thanks, Barney," he said. "You'll get a few extra points for being the geography wizard, like all the Barneys." To the class he explained, "Kelly Quinn's relatives, if born in 1669, would have been alive for the famous witch trials, which happened in Salem, Massachusetts." He clapped. "Bravo, Barney. Now you can sit."

As Charlotte stomped back to her seat, she passed me on the way and muttered, "You'll be sorry."

I looked at Charlotte Barney—my archnemesis, my next-door neighbor who ruined my surprise ninth birthday party by telling me about it, my classmate and teammate who has taunted me for years—with the most evil eyes I could make. And I said, "If you don't keep your trap shut, I WILL turn you into a frog. And I will enjoy every minute of it."

"Did you hear that?" Charlotte asked the class. "Did everyone hear that? She just threatened to turn me into a frog."

I laughed.

Frankie and Tony laughed.

Coach and Misty laughed.

Hannah and Darbie laughed.

Charlotte didn't.

No one believed her.

But *she* believed *me*.

19

A Famous TV Chef

The next day, Tuesday, we sat in homeroom while our teacher took attendance. I doodled a jack-o'-lantern on my notebook, thinking about hexing the school board and wondering what to do about Charlotte. My gaze wandered out the window and widened as a motorcade pulled into the fire lane of Alfred Nobel School.

There were three black SUVs with darkly tinted windows—the kind the FBI or secret agents use.

I said, "Maybe Darb was right about LLJ. Do you think maybe she missed a meeting with her parole officer, and now they're coming for her?"

Then a white stretch limo pulled up and parked behind the SUVs. "You think they would take her to jail in a limo?" Hannah asked.

I shook my head.

A man dressed in a pinstripe suit popped out of the limo and entered the school.

"Kelly? Kelly Quinn?" the teacher called.

"Um. Yes?"

"Attendance? Pay attention."

"Right. I'm here." It was impossible for anyone to pay attention. Now two large men in dark black suits with ear gadgets stood on either side of the limo.

Our teacher lowered the blinds and twisted them tight.

"Ohh man," we cried.

"We have work to do," she said. "Let's try attend—"

The intercom chirped with static several times; then a voice said, "Greetings, glorious Alfred Nobel School student body." It was Mr. Douglass. "I'm coming to you from the school office and all of its educational feng shui. Due to extraordinary circumstances, you are all being asked to report to the auditorium immediately."

"I bet it's the school board," I said to Hannah. "They're going to announce the official closing of F and CS and maybe other programs."

"What about planjo banjo?" Darbie asked.

"Just haven't gotten to it yet," I said.

Moments later we were in the auditorium as Mr. Douglass bounded to the center of the stage. "I have news to share!" He clapped his hands together, too excitedly for someone who was losing his job.

Kids were still taking their seats when he said, "Thanks to all of you who participated in last week's cafeteria lunch voting event."

Was he going to announce the winning recipe, the Zombie Noodles?

That was old news.

"I have an amazing surprise for you all. I can barely believe it's happening," he continued.

We all looked at one another. Maybe it wasn't about those Zombie Noodles, after all.

Mr. Douglass looked like he was about to bounce off the stage.

"It's an incredible honor to introduce the most amazing, fantabulous, lovely TV chef herself, Felice Foudini!"

The auditorium burst into applause and hollers. We all went nuts.

"Pinch me!" I yelled to Darbie.

She did, and it hurt, so I knew I wasn't dreaming. The stage lit up, and out she walked. My hero.

Felice waved and said, "Helloooooooo, Alfred Nobel School!"

More cheers.

"I am so happy to be here to personally deliver the first place prize in my recipe challenge. Would the following students please step up? Hannah Hernandez, Darbie O'Brien, Frankie and Tony Rusamano . . ." She waited while they made their way up to the steps.

Was this really happening?

How?

We hadn't even entered the challenge.

Felice continued, "LLJ?" She asked her assistant, "Is that a typo, Max?" Then to the audience: "Do we have an LLJ in the house?"

LLJ materialized from backstage. She stood almost a foot taller than Felice Foudini. "Oh, you're not a student," said Felice. "Well, thanks for being here."

LLJ nodded and grinned widely, showing a grayed-out front tooth.

"I understand the leader of this kitchen crew is Kelly Quinn!" Felice said.

My legs felt wobbly. I was shaking, but I managed to make my way to the stage. "I'm Kelly," I said. "Kelly Quinn."

Felice shook my hand. "Congratulations, Kelly. It's my pleasure to present to you and your crew this check for ten thousand dollars."

Max brought a big check from behind the stage to loud applause. We held it while Max took several pictures from every angle.

Speaking into the mic, Felice asked me, "What are you going to do with the money?"

"Well, you see Miss Foudini—I'm a huge fan, by the way—our school board has some budget issues."

"And you're going to give the money to them?"

"Um, sort of. They want to shut down our F and CS program."

"Oh, boo!" she said.

"So I'm going to use the money to help keep the F and CS program."

Felice clapped for me. "Wow!" she said. "That is very impressive and generous."

Mr. Douglass pulled a hanky from his pocket and dabbed his eyes.

Felice asked, "Is it okay if I show everyone your video?"

"Sure," I said. "Wait. I have a video?" I stepped back into line with my friends, next to Tony. Our hands brushed. And I felt a little spark.

The stage lights went dark, and sure enough a video appeared on the screen behind me. It was all of us in the cafeteria making lunch. There was a clip of me showing everyone how to make the fettuccine, LLJ piping the red icing, and Darbie rolling enchiladas while dancing. Tony was caught licking an empty bowl of cake batter. Frankie slid trays of hot enchiladas out of the oven, and Hannah sliced the layered velvety red-carpet cake.

Someone had added peppy music in the background.

Felice said, "I just love this. It was a great addition to your electronic submission."

Electronic submission?

"You and your friends look good on the big screen, don't you think?"

"Heck yeah!" Darbie said.

"In fact, I'd like you and your cooking club—I understand that it's a club—to join us on the air *live* each week until the end of the year. It will take just fifteen minutes, and we'll set up all the equipment for you. Would you be up for that?"

How could I not be up for that?

"You bet we would," I said.

"Thank you, Kelly, and thank you, Alfred Nobel School." Felice led us offstage. She was out of sight from the audience for only a second when she returned to the stage. "Remember . . . ," she called out to the auditorium.

All the kids yelled back to her. "You! Can't! Be! Too! Yummy!"

"You got it!" She flashed her signature smile.

"What do you think, Kelly?" Felice asked me.

"I think you're awesome!" I hugged her. "But I don't understand how you got my submission. We missed the deadline."

"Max?" Felice checked with her assistant.

Max produced a paper. "I have it right here. An electronic

submission. It wasn't late. It came from an Alfred Nobel School e-mail account."

"We aren't allowed to e-mail from school," I said.

At that moment a figure stepped forward from backstage, flat expression, arms crossed in front of her chest. "*Students* may not e-mail from the school account," Mrs. Eagle said.

"And," Tony said, leaning into me, "you should start reading the rest of the small print, which said that you could e-mail your submission."

"You?" I asked Tony in surprise. "You didn't tell me you did that." Then I looked at Mrs. Eagle. "And you helped?"

She nodded.

"Thank you," I said to them.

"It was no problem. I like helping out cool girls like you." As soon as he realized what he'd said, Tony blushed redder than a cranberry.

Whoa! Tony Rusamano thought I was cool.

"I think *you're* awesome too," I said to Tony, giving him a hug.

"Oh," Felice said happily. "What a great gang. I'm so psyched to have you on my show. Kelly, what will you make for your first dish?"

"Will it be before Halloween?" I asked.

"You betcha."

"I have some ideas."

20

She's Baaaaack

Sam's iScream was hopping after school.

"I thought that video was for the website," Hannah said to Tony.

"It was Mrs. Eagle's idea to include it," he said.

"Did you call her on the weekend?" I asked.

"Actually, it was weird. She called to have a shrub delivered—just one shrub. When we dropped it off, she asked about the recipe challenge. I had taken the form you filled out, because, like I had told Frankie, I was going to send it in for you that night. She knew. She really can hear everything. She asked me for it and offered to send it in with the video, which was at school."

"That was super nice of her," I said.

Frankie said, "I'll bring her some of my mom's cannoli."

"What are we gonna do for the first show?" Hannah asked.

"I thought we could do a whole Halloween thing and make the Zombie Noodles. Even dress up with black capes and hats."

"Like witches," Frankie said.

"Right," Darbie said. "Exactly like witches."

We laughed, but the boys didn't seem to think it was as funny as we did.

Sam delivered our Swirleys. "On the house!" he said. "To celebrate."

"Thanks, Sam. This is a perfect day." I sat with my back to the door and dove into my Black and White Swirley. "It couldn't possibly get any better."

"Um," Hannah said. "There's one thing that might make it better." Hannah stared over my shoulder at the door.

Sam cried out, "Ida! You're back!"

I spun around. "Señora P!"

We all ran over to hug her. Hannah, Darbie, and I started filling her in, talking at the same time: "F and CS," "the school board," "Felice Foudini," "agave," "Coach Richards," "Charlotte," "frogs," "Salem—"

She held up her hands. "I know. I know. I know everything."

"How?" I asked.

"My old friend Kai Eagle called me. You cannot hide anything from her." She pointed to her ears.

"Well, that's efficient," Darbie said. "You're totally up to speed."

"But we're not," Hannah said. "Where have you been?"

"Mexico," she said. "To visit my family and get some more spices." She sat down to tell us more.

That's when there was a pecking noise outside Sam's window. He cracked the door open, and a crow the size of a turkey buzzard flew in and landed on Señora P's shoulder. Señora P gave him a nuzzle.

"I missed you too, Sweetie." She fiddled in the pocket of her muumuu and pulled out a kernel of corn for it.

"*Caw!*" Sweetie replied to her.

She patted its black head and let out a long sigh.

"What's wrong?" Darbie asked. "Didn't you have a nice visit?"

"I did," she said. "It's what I found when I came back. I went through my mail and found this." Again she reached into the depth of a muumuu pocket, and a letter emerged.

Frankie looked at the outside. "It's from Delaware Commercial Realty Company, LLC."

"That is my landlord. It is who I pay my rent to."

Frankie took the letter out and read a section. "'Due to

the rising costs of maintaining your building and the high demand for storefront property in the northern Delaware area, starting November first, your rent will be increased. Please sign the enclosed revised rental agreement and return with your next rent payment by November fifth.'"

"That stinks," Darbie said. "Stinks like Gorgonzola on a hot summer day."

"I cannot pay that amount. I can just make the rent as it is. There are not many customers left who are looking for the spices I offer. I think I will have to close my store and move back to Mexico."

"Is that what you want?" I asked her.

"No! I love it here. I love my store."

"And look at this." Hannah pointed to the signature on the letter. "I guess the poisoned apple doesn't fall far from the tree."

21

A Win-Win

The next day was a beautiful, sunny, crisp fall day, which unfortunately meant that we had soccer.

"This is gonna work," Hannah said. She whipped out a whole-wheat pretzel. "Señora P gave me Cedronian lavender. Real fresh. I sprinkled the pretzel with it. This should calm Coach."

While the team stretched, Hannah put her soccer bag down on a bench and said, to no one in particular, "Oh, look at that. I forgot I had one of those superhealthy one-hundred-percent-organic whole-wheat pretzels from that nature place in Philadelphia. Too bad I'm about to run around for practice, and I don't want to eat right now. It'll be stale later. Oh well. I'll throw it away." She walked right past Coach Richards on her way to the trash can, giving him a good view of the pretzel.

He said, "Hold it right there, Hernandez. I'll take that off your hands."

"You want it?"

"Give it here." He took the pretzel and ate it in three bites, washing it down with a green cold-pressed juice. "Love whole wheat." He flexed his biceps. "And so do these bad boys. Now get out there and warm up."

Hannah joined the girls. "Mission accomplished."

"He certainly looks calm," I said.

We studied him as we passed the ball around.

He took his cell phone out of his pocket and tapped the screen a bit. His expression quickly changed. Whatever he read made his face turn red and his jaw clench. He put the phone away, slammed his empty green-juice bottle into the trash can, and lifted his foot to stretch one quad and then the other. "Okay, girls. Follow me. We're gonna run to the lifting gym and pump some iron today. Cross-training is the key to success."

He took off. Fast. And we scurried to keep up with him.

"Another text from Coach Madden?" I asked.

"That'd be my guess," Hannah said.

"I don't even lift a curling iron." Darbie pointed to her curly hair.

"He's clearly immune to the powers of the potions," Hannah said.

Charlotte ran up behind us. "Nice try," she said. "But you aren't even good witches. If you had a member of your club who was good at science and chemistry, I wonder if you'd have better results?"

"We're totally closed to new members," Darbie said. "Only three aprons."

"In that case, I wonder what Coach would think if I told him you've been tricking him into eating foods with magical ingredients?"

"I'll tell him you're a real jokester and he'll laugh at you, just like he did last time," I said.

"Even if I showed him these?" She pulled her phone out of the waistband of her shorts and showed us pictures she'd taken of the book. "Do you think I wouldn't have given myself a little insurance? Do you think I just fell off the turnip truck? Really, girls, you continue to underestimate me. Face it—I am always going to be one step ahead of you." She looked at the pictures on her phone. "They would be great on social media; then everyone can potion everyone. Think people will believe me then? And since the only place people can get these funny ingredients is in La Cocina, your friend's store will get more business, and then maybe she can pay her rent."

She ran past us, then turned around and called backward, "It's what I call a win-win."

22

The Most Romantic Time of the Year

After lifting in the gym, we dragged our aching bodies up the street to La Cocina.

"Under 'evil' in the dictionary is a picture of Charlotte Barney," I said, huffing and puffing as we slowly made our way to the store.

"I can think of a few other words that would also be above her photo," Hannah added. "I think we need Memory Maker Part Two?"

"Sounds like a plan," I said. "I can't remember it offhand. We'll have to look it up and see what ingredient we need."

Darbie lagged behind on our quarter-mile trek. "Now

in addition to my legs hurting, so do my glutes, schmutes, pecs, schmecks, lats, and schmats. Why do allllll those muscles need to be strong?"

"Richards is out of control," I agreed. "And so is Charlotte."

"Don't forget about the greedy landlord," Darbie said.

Hannah said, "For Coach, if we can't get him to chill with a potion, we have to get Madden to lighten up. Let's try to potion her. I'll deliver it personally."

"What if we make things worse?" Darbie asked.

"Can it possibly get worse?" Hannah asked.

"Oh, let's see. He could put us in camo and take us out to the state park and make us do wilderness survival training with no food, no shoes, no cell phone," Darbie said. "Did I mention no food? And then he'll make us eat off the land, stuff like roaches and toads, probably without cooking them."

"Oh, come on. How would that improve our game?" I asked, then I thought for a second and added, "Ya think?"

"A rivalry is a serious thing, Kell," Hannah said. "It baffles the best scientists in the world."

"But roaches?" I asked.

They both shrugged like anything was possible.

"We have a lot of people to manage right now," Hannah said. "What if we divide and conquer? Why don't you take Richards and Madden," she said to Darbie.

"Got it."

Just then a Rusamano Landscaping truck drove past us. Frankie and Tony were in the back. "What happened?" Frankie yelled. "You're walking like old ladies!" The truck pulled away, but not before Tony made eye contact with me and waved.

"Oooo, did you see that?" Hannah asked. "Love is in the air."

"I saw it." I blushed and changed the subject. "Let's bring Señora P a Swirley—maybe it'll cheer her up."

We popped into Sam's Super iScream to grab cups of frozen perfection, then entered La Cocina for the first time in weeks. Nothing had changed, except maybe there was more dust.

Strings of shells hung from the doorknob and knocked together as the door inched closed behind us, cutting us off from the rest of Wilmington. Tinted windows blocked the sunlight. A big stuffed, dead bear welcomed us into this alternate universe.

I didn't know if it was the cold, ice creamy heaven in my hand, or that Señora P hadn't turned her heat on yet, but I felt a frigid breeze on the back of my knees.

"We've been here so many times, and I still can't get used to him watching us," Hannah said about a moose head hanging on the wall, its shiny glass eyes staring at us.

"He's a total creepasaurus," Darbie confirmed.

We headed toward a curtain made of beads that separated the front of the store from the back. On the way, I scanned the shelves of spices—hundreds of little bottles filled with dusts, elixirs, extracts, and syrups. Some were in golden or greenish or bluish jars; others were in vials capped with corks. The glass was so thick on some of the bottles, you could hardly see inside. On the bottom of each was a small handwritten label.

When we made it to the back, I called toward the beads that hung like a waterfall, "Señora? Are you here? It's us!"

Her hand swiped the beads to the side. *"Hola, niñas."* Señora Perez was small, shorter than Darbie, who was the third shortest kid in our grade. She had black-and-gray-streaked hair piled high on top of her head. And sitting on her shoulder was her crow, whose feathers shone like he'd been spritzed with olive oil. He hadn't, of course; he just had greasy feathers, like all crows.

"Come back." She waved us along and sighed. "Sit with me." Her voice dripped with gloom.

The first time I'd come back here, I'd imagined I'd find heavy burgundy tapestry drapes, crystal balls, Tarot cards, Victorian chairs with high backs, Persian rugs, and mysterious fortune-teller-type stuff.

Instead, it was an old office. The floor was linoleum, lifted up and torn off in several spots. There was one set of furniture—a decrepit metal kitchen table with folding chairs open on each side. There was a small counter space with a hot plate, some silver canisters, and a vase filled with utensils. On the wall, a mesh metal tea ball dangled from a hook. A small shelf above the counter held a few cracked teacups, chipped plates, mismatched bowls, and a kettle. There was no crystal ball to be found.

Darbie handed Señora P the Swirley. "We got you Salted-Caramel Chocolate Explosion. Sam thought you'd like it."

Señora P smiled. Swirleys can do that to people. "He knows me so well." She took the cup and sipped.

Señora P lifted the plastic lid and held it up for the crow. He stuck his beak in, then pulled back. He wasn't the Swirley type.

We all groaned as we lowered our aching bodies onto the metal chairs.

"That soccer coach still a *problema*?" Señora Perez asked.

"A potion *problemo*," Darbie clarified.

"The lavender didn't work," Hannah said. "It's like he's immune to the potion. Is that possible?"

"I suppose anything is possible. RS knew the most about the magic. Every group has a leader, and she was ours. She kept a secret from us. Many years after that summer, I got a message from her that she'd written down that secret and hidden it."

"Do you know where?" I asked.

"Well, not exactly, but I have a clue. She said she hid it inside the tomb of my oldest relative."

"That sounds like a cemetery," I said.

"*Sí*," Señora P said.

"That's not rocket science," Hannah said. "If we find the cemetery plot for her oldest relative, we'll find the secret. There can't be many cemeteries in Wilmington."

"Let's do it," Darbie said. "Then we can master the potions, fix Coach's problem, buy this building from Mr. Barney, and turn Charlotte into a frog,"

"But," I said, "we would have to know who RS is in order to find her relatives. And what if her relatives aren't from Delaware?"

Darbie asked Señora P, "This would be so much easier if you would just tell us who RS is. Why not just save us the time, huh?"

"I cannot. I made a *promesa*."

"*Promesa*, schmomesa," Darbie said, then noisily slurped the end of her Swirley. "And I schmomesa that this is darn good stuff, cross my heart." She made an imaginary *X* on her heart with her finger.

We all laughed. I took another sip of my Swirley and brought up a topic that wasn't quite as funny.

"What's happening with Mr. Barney and the property company?" I asked.

Señora Perez's mood immediately went from Swirley happiness to gloom. "I really don't know how I can afford the new rent. I'm going to close and just retire in Mexico."

"Oh no. You can't," I protested.

Hannah added, "Wilmington needs you. We need you."

Our phones chirped with a text.

"It's from Charlotte," I said.

23

Our Most Major Hex

The text said, **You have twenty-four hours to offer me membership, or the recipes go viral.**

We explained Memory Maker Part One to Señora Perez. She said, "I know Memory Maker Part Two because I wrote that one." She stood, the crow immediately landing on her shoulder to come along for the ride, and walked through the beaded curtain to the front of the store, where she reached for a bottle. But it was too high, so Hannah got it for her. It was dark amber. She unscrewed the cap and showed a dropper. "This is

Cedronian tryptophanberry elixir. Very powerful. Mix it into a lotion, and it is absorbed through the skin."

"What does it do?"

"It will put her into a walking trance. She will go through the motions of a regular person, but she will be entranced and do what you tell her."

"This is perfect! I love it," Darbie said. "We will control Charlotte Barney. This is going to be hours and hours of fun. Can we go do it right now?"

"Um," Hannah said. "Let's think about this one a little bit."

"Yeah," I agreed.

"Are you kidding me?" Darbie asked. "You're not sure if you want to control Charlotte? Do I have to remind you of every mean thing she has ever done to us? I don't think I have enough time for that."

"Don't get me wrong," I said. "I love the idea, but this is the biggest hex we've ever considered."

"The Return could be huge," Hannah added.

Darbie raised her hand. "I'll take that one. I know it's not my turn, but bring on that Return. Any price is worth entrancing Charlotte Barney."

"We have twenty-four hours, let's at least sleep on it," I said.

"In the meantime," Señora P said, "you can try this for your coach." She pushed bottles around, perched her reading glasses on the tip of her nose, and read the bottoms until she found one she wanted. "This should drive away hostility."

Hannah twisted open the cap and poured a few of the pointy seeds into her palm. "How am I going to get him to eat one of these?"

"He does not eat it," Señora P said.

24

Cloves and Bug Spray

The next day at soccer we ran up and down the hill, which no longer had grass because we'd stomped it all out.

Charlotte and Misty slowed down so that we could catch up to them.

"Oh, such a shame about your friend's store," Misty said. "But the town can really use a Sneaker Studio in that little strip mall."

"Your dad already has a new tenant ready to move in?" I asked.

"We Barneys move fast." Charlotte glanced at her watch.

"There's no telling what might happen over the next four hours." She sped up to get ahead of us, then turned and called back, "Hannah, you wanna pick up your pace and run with me? Coach is picking the starters for the next game based on who does best with this workout."

Hannah looked at Darbie and me. She really wanted to be a starting player and was much better than us.

"Go on," I said. "You should start."

Darbie added, "Don't want to hold you back, Han-Flimflam—" She was going to say more, but she couldn't find the breath.

Hannah jogged ahead to keep up with Charlotte and Misty.

"I hate Charlotte." Darbie had no trouble finding air for that. "What did you decide about the lotion?"

I didn't answer her, because I was still a chicken about it. "How about we start with cloves? You have it?"

She patted her pocket.

At our water break I asked her, "Now? You have a plan?"

"I'm the man with the plan, Kell-Bell-Farmer-in-the-Dell."

I laughed—I was probably in the minority, but I thought Darbie was funny, and she never jazzed up my name. She probably did it to Hannah just to annoy her.

Darbie sipped her water and walked around casually, slowly getting closer to Coach Richards. She reached into her pocket, and I saw her carefully position the clove in her hand so that the pointy part was poking out.

Coach Richards flipped pages on his clipboard, studying plays and lineup notes.

That's when Darbie made her move. She slapped Coach on the back of his arm.

"Ouch!" he screamed.

All the girls on the team looked at him.

He said, "What the—?"

"A bug," Darbie said matter-of-factly. "I got it. It was a big sucker too. Those characters carry all kinds of viruses."

I added, "It is crazy buggy here today."

He rubbed his arm.

"It feels like it bit me," he said, but he couldn't see the back of his arm. He looked at his hand. "Viruses?"

Darbie looked down in the grass. "Oh, I see him. He's the harmless kind."

"How do you know?"

Darbie whispered to him, "I'm kind of a bug lover. I read about them. Look at pictures and stuff. It's my secret nerd hobby. Don't tell the other girls."

Darbie walked over to me. "Mission complete."

I was impressed. Poking Coach with a clove sounded impossible, but there we had it.

We watched him carefully. He hopped up onto a bench and called out, "Gather round. I have a surprise for you."

"He's gonna end practice early," I said. "I can feel it."

"And give us tomorrow off." Darbie high-fived me. "We are so good at this stuff."

"Listen up," Coach said. "I was able to borrow these vests from my friend at the police academy." He held one up. "They are filled with ten pounds of weights. And there is one for each of you. You put it on like this." He slid it over his head. "And then you lunge like this." He jumped off the bench and put one foot in front of the other and bent his other knee to the ground, then moved that foot forward and put the other knee to the ground.

"I drew a path with white chalk starting at the parking lot and going all around school and the surrounding neighborhood. Get to it." The rest of the team started sliding vests over their heads. "And if you don't come back with your knees scraped, you did it wrong."

Hannah joined us. "What are you waiting for? Poke him with that clove."

"She did," I said.

"Maybe," Darbie said, "we aren't that good at this stuff."

"Ugh," Hannah said. "What are we doing wrong?"

The team started following the chalk path, except Charlotte, who dawdled and played with her phone.

"Barney, get moving!" Coach yelled at her.

"You got it, Coach. I just need to post this one thing. I was going to do it later, but you know what they say, there's no time like the present."

I did my best act of being calm, cool, and collected. I turned away from the rest of the girls, picked up the three remaining vests, and handed two to Darbie and Hannah. I whispered, "Act totally normal."

They each took a vest.

I smiled and asked Darbie, "You have the elixir?"

She nodded.

To Hannah, I asked, "You have the bug spray?"

She nodded.

"Get them."

Charlotte said, "I'm getting ready to do it. . . ."

We ignored her.

"Twist open the bug spray."

Hannah did.

"Add the elixir."

Darbie poured the liquid into the bug spray container, then screwed the top tightly to seal it.

Then, more loudly, I said, "These vests are heavy. . . . What!? Man, I just got bit again! I hate these bugs. Can I use your bug spray?"

Hannah gave me hers.

Charlotte said, "All I have to do is push this button."

I walked over to her with the bug spray and confronted her. Charlotte loves a confrontation. "You know, Charlotte—"

"What, Kelly Quinn? All I need to hear is that my

membership is confirmed, and I don't have to post anything anywhere."

"I was going to say, that it's very buggy today." And I
sprayed the bug spray all over her neck and arms.

"Kelly Quinn! I don't need bug spray!"

I said, "Yes, you do."

She repeated back, "Yes, I do."

25
Finding RS

The next morning Mom made pancakes. Bud poked holes in his and lay it on his face like a mask. (Boys can be so gross.) He laughed so hard that the pancake flopped off his face and onto the floor, where it sat for only a hot second before my dog, Rosey, grabbed it and ran out. Rosey was supposed to be on a diet, on account of Bud giving her so much table food, so I chased her down to get the pancake.

On our pancake chase, we bumped into the hall table, knocking the mail to the floor. By the time I got to Rosey, the pancake was gone and she looked like it had never even existed. I pointed to her because I knew the truth. "Don't do that again," I said to her sternly. She pretended she had no idea what I was talking about, but she didn't fool me. She knew.

I picked up the mail, including a few letters and things that weren't for us. One was for Regina Silvers. I always thought Mrs. Silvers's first name was Gina, but I'd never thought about it. As I studied it more, the initials jumped out at me. RS.

RS. KE.

Could Mrs. Silvers be RS?

Suddenly some things made sense:

The spices in her yard—maybe she was trying to grow her own potion-able spices.

Maybe her knee healed so quickly because she used a little magical ingredient on it.

Her age—it seemed to match with Mrs. Eagle and Señora Perez. Could they have been best friends that summer so long ago and made the Secret Recipe Book?

I tingled all over, because it all fit together.

"I'm leaving!" I called into the kitchen. I ran past my bus stop and continued to the next one a few streets away, where Hannah and Darbie were waiting. I guess all that soccer training paid off, because I got there really fast without even breaking a sweat.

"What are you doing?" Darbie asked.

"Silvers," I said. "Regina Silvers. *RS*." I showed them the unopened letter.

Their mouths flapped open.

"Unbelievable," Darbie said.

"It was literally right in front of us—her house is across the street, right in front of yours—the whole time," Hannah said. "But why would her book be in your attic?"

"Remember?" I asked. "Her basement flooded, and we've been storing her stuff?"

They nodded.

"For as long as I can remember, you've thought she was a witch," Hannah said.

"I said that because she was a mean old lady. But she's nice now that her knee is better."

"Subconsciously, you knew all along," Darbie said.

"I don't think so," I said.

"That's how the subconscious works," Darbie explained. "If you'd known, it wouldn't be *sub*. It's the *sub* part."

Maybe she was right. Who knew about the *sub* part, really?

We got on the bus and saw Charlotte and Misty in the back. Usually we sit as far away from them as possible, but today Hannah kept walking toward the back of the bus and sat down just two rows away.

Darbie sat next to her and whispered, "What are you doing?"

"I want to hear how this whole trance thing is panning out," Hannah said. "Shh. Listen."

We eavesdropped on their conversations.

Misty said, "You're quiet today. Everything okay?" When Charlotte didn't respond, Misty added, "Are you mad at me?"

I turned around and said, "She's not mad at you, are you, Charlotte?"

"No," Charlotte said.

Misty asked, "Were you listening to our private conversation, Kelly Quinn?" It was like she was trying to sound like Charlotte.

"Charlotte doesn't mind, do you, Charlotte?"

"No. It's fine."

"Tell Misty why you're so quiet. Go on, tell her how you really feel about the possibility of La Cocina closing. You're sad about it."

Charlotte told Misty, "I am. I'm sad that the store might close."

Darbie whispered to me, "Tell her that she wants me to start in the next soccer game, and she's gonna tell Coach about it."

I said, "Charlotte, remember when you told me how well Darbie was doing at practices and you were going to tell Coach to start her instead of Misty, who's been looking a little out of shape?"

"I do," she said. "I'll tell him that today."

"Out of shape!" Misty balked. "Look at these calves." She propped her leg on the seat in front of her and flexed.

"Oh my God, I love this," Darbie said. "Tell her to croak like a frog. I'm going to video it on my phone." Darbie took her phone out of her backpack. "Oh no," she said.

"What?"

"It's dead. Well, not totally dead." She held it out for us to see. It was the *World Book Encyclopedia* website, but wherever she touched, nothing happened. It was just a frozen home page.

"Try turning it off and back on again," Hannah said.

Darbie pushed a side button. "It won't even turn off."

"I bet it's your Return. For Memory Maker," I said.

"I'm addicted. I admit it." She put her hand on her heart. "I think I'm having a panic attack," Darbie said. "I'd rather have uncontrollable gas than go a day without my phone."

"Uh, no you wouldn't," I said. "That's not fair to any of us."

"How am I going to survive without my phone?"

"You can borrow mine, if you need to," I said.

"Okay. Give it to me so I can record her croaking. And if you can get her to hop, that would shore up the viral-ability of this puppy."

She held out her hand, but I didn't give her my phone.

"I thought you were going to share," she said.

"We can't make her croak and hop. That would be so obvious, and people might actually believe her claim that I'm a witch," I said.

"Fine. Well I need a deed to do," Darbie said.

"I won't be able to get one from the box until after school," I said.

"Can't we make one up?" she asked.

"We've never tried that before," I said. "But maybe it will work. We probably need someone to keep an eye on you-know-who today." I nodded toward Charlotte. "You know, to make sure she doesn't do anything crazy."

"Or dangerous," Hannah said. "I'm not feeling good about this hex."

"Oh, relax, Hannah-Hollaback. Let's have a little fun with it." Then Darbie added, "She's been terrorizing us for how long?"

I said, "Okay, but you stay close to her today."

"That's a sacrifice if I ever heard one," Darbie said.

When the bus arrived at school, Misty walked past us to get off first. When Charlotte followed, I said into her ear, "Go have a completely normal regular day at school. Act normal."

She headed out, but then I pulled her back. "Except be nice. To everyone."

"That should be fun to watch," Darbie said.

"Keep an eye on her," I reminded Darbie.

"I'm on it."

"And," Hannah said. "Today. After school. We're cemetery hopping. We're finding the crypt of Mrs. Silvers's oldest relative."

Darbie said, "Um, the thing is that *subconsciously* I don't like crypts."

"If you know that, then it's not sub," I said.

"True. Then I just don't like them. Consciously."

"Well," Hannah said. "Consciously, you're going with us."

This Ain't Scooby-Doo

We got off the bus at three o'clock.

"How was she today?" I asked Darbie.

"Everyone was shocked that she said nice things to them. I told them that she'd had a near-death experience last night, nearly choking on a walnut, but that I'd saved her life, and that she'd pledged to be a better person. They bought it, and they all think I'm a hero." She took out her phone. "Ugh. Still dead. And I hung out with her all day."

"We'll go get something from the box in a minute," I said. Then I asked Hannah, "What's the cemetery plan?"

Hannah took her iPad out of her pack. "I downloaded

a map of the town and circled the cemeteries. Turns out there are a few more than I thought. Four total."

"That seems like a lot of hallowed ground to cover," I said.

"Ruh-roh," Darbie said. "We are not splitting up and looking for clues. Let's get that straight right now. This ain't *Scooby-Doo*. You'd think they would notice that every time they do that, a Creeper finds Shaggy and Scooby and chases them. In this scenario, since there are only three of us, I'm Shaggy *and* Scooby. So, the Cemetery Creeper is definitely going to find *me* and chase *me*." She added, "You'd both be fine."

"No one is splitting us up," I said. "Right?" I asked Hannah.

"That won't be necessary. We only need to go to one."

"How do you know which one?" I asked.

"I submitted a form to each of these—an electronic request asking if the Silverses were buried there." She added, "It's pubic information."

"And you found the right one?" I asked.

Hannah pointed to the map. "Ye Olde Wilmington Graveyard."

"Then let's get ready for an outing."

We started walking down the street to my house.

Darbie was quiet until she said, "Hannah would be Velma. And Kell, you're Daphne."

We dropped off our backpacks, I picked a deed for Darbie—"Do something kind for an elderly person"—and

Darbie loaded herself down with snacks and put on her Rollerblades. By the time we were ready to leave my house, it was nearly four o'clock.

"I don't know why you can't just walk," Hannah said.

"This is way more fun. And we could get there twice as fast if you did it too," Darbie said. "You know it's getting dark earlier, and I do NOT want to be in Ye Olde Wilmington Graveyard after dark. We can't afford to waste time in transit."

Hannah and I looked at each other, and a second later, we were both in Rollerblades too.

We rolled past Charlotte's house. She was out front practicing juggling a soccer ball.

She waved. "Hannah Hernandez, you look pretty today. And Kelly, you are a wonderful neighbor. Is your little brother home? Maybe he and I can play a board game."

Darbie said, "What about me? Don't you have something nice to say to me?"

"Thanks for saving my life, Darbie O'Brien. I don't know how I'll ever repay you."

"Any time," Darbie said.

"Where are you guys off to?" Charlotte asked.

Darbie spun her body around to skate backward and said to Charlotte, "Out and about. That's how we roll. Ha! Get it?" She turned back around and said more softly, probably to herself, "Man, I'm funny."

Hannah didn't look like she was having too much fun, tottering along on her skates. Hannah was good at pretty much everything she tried, so when there was something she wasn't great at, look out.

"I don't know if this is really much faster," Hannah said.

Darbie yelled to her phone. "Hey, Darbie's phone, how much faster is roller-skating than walking?" No response. "Drat," she said.

I said, "You're right about the dark." The sun was getting low, and it was getting cold. "We have to hustle."

Maybe we hadn't thought through the footwear as thoroughly as we should have, because when we switched from pavement to graveyard grass, we had to sort of march along, which looked funny and was tough on the ankles.

"This place is bigger than I thought it would be," Hannah said. "I think we have to—"

"Oh, lemme guess," Darbie said. "Shag and Scoob, you go that way."

I said, "Sorry, Darb, but there's no way we'll be able to cover all this ground if we stick together."

Just then there was a crackling of leaves behind some trees nearby.

"Did you hear that?" Darbie asked. "The Creeper isn't waiting until I'm alone. Bold move."

"It's probably a squirrel or something," Hannah said,

and verbally laid out the sections we would each search, so that we wouldn't miss any headstones and we wouldn't overlap.

There was another crackle.

"Did you hear that?" Darbie asked again. "Maybe we should come back when it's light out."

"Don't be a baby," Hannah said. "We can do this."

Just then a pinecone zoomed at us, barely missing Darbie's head.

"Luckily the Creeper has bad aim," Darbie said.

Hannah said, "That was no Creeper."

"No," I confirmed, then yelled, "Just creeps! Two of them!"

Frankie and Tony came out from behind a tree, laughing hysterically.

"You following us?" Hannah asked.

"Yup," Frankie confessed without a smidgen of regret. "And, Hannah, you clomp around like a newborn giraffe on those things. I didn't think there was anything you weren't awesome at."

Hannah glared at him. "Oh, shut up."

"Since you're here, as weird as it is that you stalked us, you can help us find the tomb of Mrs. Silvers's oldest relative before it gets dark," Darbie said.

"This is when a normal person would ask why you're in search of an old witch's ancestor, but we're not going to do that." Frankie asked Tony, "Are we?"

"Nope," Tony agreed.

"Good," Darbie said. "Frankie, you can be Fred, and, Tony, I guess you'll be Shaggy. But, wait, that leaves me as . . . well, whatever. Let's just look."

"And fast," I added. "I really don't want to be in here when it's dark."

We went off in the directions Hannah identified and studied the names on the tombstones and mausoleums. Tony tagged along with me. I was nearly convinced that he liked me without Love Bug Juice.

"What are we looking for?" he asked.

"A letter," I replied. "It's hidden in the tomb of Mrs. Silvers's oldest relative."

"That makes perfect sense," he said.

"I found it!" Darbie called. "One point for the Scoob." She patted her own back.

Racing there on Rollerblades in the grass wasn't easy, but I did my best. I kind of half ran, half rolled. Tony grabbed my elbow at one point when I nearly fell. I smiled when he did that.

We gathered around the tombstone.

Darbie read to us. "'Beulah Silvers. 1699 to 1755. Beloved mother, wife, schoolteacher.'" She slid her phone out of her back pocket. "I wanna get a pic of this." She aimed the phone and—"Drat. Still dead."

"Where's the letter?" I asked. I felt all around the top

and edge of the tombstone and the grass under it. "It's just a rock. How are we going to find a letter in a rock?"

"What about one of those cement buildings?" Frankie asked.

"None of them are Silverses," Hannah said. "This has to be it. Keep feeling around, Kell. Is there a crack? Or a latch that slides a drawer or something?"

I continued to feel, and then I even knocked on the rock, trying to find a hollow space. "It's solid," I said, then added, "We better go. We only have a little bit of daylight left."

Then we heard a noise. It wasn't someone walking on leaves or throwing pinecones. This was the distinct sound of lock tumblers clicking into place.

The big, strong, metal lock of the Wilmington Cemetery gate closing for the night.

Boys in the Know

"Oh no," I said. "Is it locked?"

Frankie and Tony ran ahead of us because they could run on the grass faster than we could march-skate.

A cemetery van drove down Olde Wilmington Road, away from the cemetery. Frankie shook the gate and called after the van, but it didn't turn back. He shook the gate again. "That's about as locked as locked gets," he confirmed.

Hannah looked like she was going to be sick. "My dad is gonna kill me," she said.

"Let's not exaggerate, Hannah-Hippie-Hopscotch," Darbie said.

"Fine. I'll be in a lot of trouble. Okay?"

"This is why one of us needs an older sibling," I said. "To rescue us in times like this."

"Don't worry. Since I'm a hero and everything, I can call my cousin Rex. He'll be here in a second." Darbie took out her phone and—"I keep forgetting this thing isn't working."

"We've gotcha covered, girls," Frankie said. "Tone, you want to make the call?"

"I already texted—"

"Oh, rub it in," Darbie said.

Tony finished, "The cavalry is on the way."

"Now would be a perfect time for you to tell us what's going on," Frankie said.

"Going on?" I asked, and made my best confused face and looked at Hannah.

Hannah said, "Going on? What's going on?"

Darbie added, "Don't know what you mean. Why can't three girls roller-skate to a cemetery without getting the third degree?"

Finally, a big white pickup truck with the Rusamano Landscaping logo pulled up in front of the gate.

"Hey, Pete!" Frankie called.

"Yo, Pete-ster!" Tony called.

Pete-ster? Maybe Tony was starting to relax around me.

Darbie asked Tony, "That Pete-ster doesn't look strong enough to break this iron fence. What is he, like, seventy or eighty years old?"

"Nah," Tony said. "He just has gray hair. He's like thirty-five-ish."

"Um, that's practically elderly," Darbie remarked. Then she called, "Hey, Darbie's phone, how old is considered elderly?"

No answer from her phone.

"Drat. I miss it so much. It's like withdrawal."

"What happened to it?" Frankie asked.

"Payback," she said.

"Your phone isn't working because it's mad at you?"

"Something like that. You figure you save someone's life when they're about to choke on a walnut that karma would be on your side, you know? But not in my world."

Pete, a Rusamano Landscaping employee covered in mulch, came to the iron gate and asked, "How do you get yourselves into these jams?"

Darbie asked Pete, "You gonna do like a Hulk thing and stretch these iron bars?"

Pete grabbed a ladder off the truck and slid it over the fence. "This is probably easier, plus I won't rip my shirt by turning big and green."

Darbie said, "I like you, Pete-ster."

Tony climbed up and jumped down to the ground on the

other side. Then he went to the truck to get a second ladder so that we wouldn't have to jump down in skates, which would probably have meant broken legs, ankles, and knees.

Frankie climbed to the top of the first ladder and said to Hannah, "Okay, come on."

She tried to step on the first rung with skates. It wasn't going to work. She took them off and tried again, but Frankie moved the ladder so she couldn't step up.

"What the heck, Frankie?"

"Tell us about this letter business. What are you really doing here looking for Mrs. Silvers's relatives' tombstones?"

"Or what?" she asked. "You're gonna leave us here?"

"You wouldn't dare," Darbie said.

"You can't be serious," I added.

He pulled the ladder up. "Our work here is done, Pete," he called over to the truck.

Pete started the engine.

"Fine," I said. "We found a Secret Recipe Book that makes potions and we've been giving them to people, but we can't seem to make Coach stop these insane workouts he's been giving us because he's afraid the other team will beat us; and Charlotte found out and videoed the Book and threatened to make it viral, so we entranced her; and in order to figure out all the rules of magic, we need to find the original authors of the Book; we have two—Señora Perez and Mrs. Eagle—but we need the third, whose initials are RS, which we thought was Mrs. Silvers, Regina Silvers; and the legend says that she hid a letter about the magic in the tomb of her oldest relative, which is why we're here, but it isn't here, so maybe she isn't RS after all."

The boys didn't say anything for a beat. Then it was Tony who spoke first. Of all the things he could have said, he asked, "Why didn't you just ask Mrs. Silvers instead of the cemetery-hopping?"

We fell silent. Darbie said, "Well, *that* makes more sense when you put it that way."

Hound Dog

"W hy didn't we think of that?" Hannah asked when we got back to my house.

"It's not like Mrs. Silvers and I were really having a ton of deep conversations here," I explained. "I've only just started talking with her a tiny bit in the last few weeks. How do you think she would feel if I asked, 'Hey, can you tell me where your relatives are buried?' And she'd be like, 'Why do you want to know?' Then I'd say, 'Well, because I figured you wrote a book of potions, and rumor has it that's where the last rule of magic is hidden. Did you write a potion book when you were a kid?'" I gave Hannah a look.

"Yeah. It sounds weird," Hannah agreed.

"But I thought of another way we could find out for sure," I said. "Why don't we get Mrs. Silvers and Señora P together, and we can see if they know each other. You know, if they talk about old times."

"That sounds good," Darbie said. "But . . . how are we going to get them together?"

"Mrs. Silvers has been walking a lot. I thought we could get her to walk up the street to La Cocina."

"And how are you going to do that?" Hannah asked.

"With this." I held up my mom's old gadget—a compact CD player—and earbuds. "I'll give her this and tell her how she can wear it while she walks, and I'll offer to go with her up to the street to show her how it works. You guys will be there and invite us in to La Cocina to see something."

"And, presto! We'll see if the two old cats know each other," Darbie said. "I like it, except that *I'm* going to give the elderly cat the Discman and walk her up the street, and my phone will work and that'll be that."

The next morning Darbie went to Mrs. Silvers's house, while Hannah and I went to La Cocina. We gave Darbie my phone and dialed Hannah's. She put it in her pocket so we could hear the whole thing.

She knocked on the heavy wooden door with the brass knocker.

Mrs. Silvers answered it. "Hi, Darbie. Do you have mail for me too?"

"No, actually, I brought you this."

"What is it?"

"I saw that you've been walking, that your knee is a lot better. You put these in your ears like this, and it plays music. I have an Elvis CD in there now."

"Oh, I like Elvis, but I don't know. I don't do well with those electronic gizmos."

"Well, I can show you. Let's give it a try."

"That sounds like it would be all right. Let me get a sweater."

There was a second of silence. Then Darbie said, "Like this. How does that feel?"

"It feels okay. Like I have something in my ears."

"Perfect. Now, can you hear the music?"

"I can! It's 'Hound Dog.' I love this song."

"Is it too loud?"

"No. It's just right."

Each time a new song came on, Mrs. Silvers announced it. About five minutes later, we saw them coming up the street. As planned, Hannah and I came outside La Cocina.

I said, "Hi there! You wanna come in and look at the cauldron that Señora P is going to let us borrow for the Felice Foudini show?"

"I would love to see it," Darbie said. "Wouldn't you?" she asked Mrs. Silvers. "And you can sit for a minute and rest before we walk back home."

"Oh, okay. That sounds good."

I held the door open for her. She sat in an elaborately carved wooden chair with a worn golden cushion.

"Have you ever been here?" Hannah asked Mrs. Silvers.

"Oh sure."

Darbie said, "I think I'll get Señora Perez to help with the thing. The stuff."

"That's a very good idea," I said. "You should."

"Do you know Señora Perez?" Hannah asked her.

Mrs. Silvers nodded. "Of course, this is a small town."

Her expression didn't let on anything.

Señora P, with that crow, shuffled out behind Darbie.

"*Hola*," she said to Mrs. Silvers. "Was there something I could help you with?"

"Me? Oh, no. I'm just taking a little rest. It was this one"—she indicated Darbie—"that needed you for something."

"You do?" she asked Darbie.

Darbie stuttered. "Uh, yeah. I wanted to ask you about something. A thing. Some stuff. But now I forget."

Señora P eyed Darbie knowingly. She tilted her head as if to say, *You're up to something*. She handed her a small paper bag in which I figured there were Moon Honey drops. "Well, let me know when you remember." With that, Señora P and her crow headed back toward the beaded curtain.

"Wait," I said. "I wondered if Mrs. Silvers went to the same pool you did when you were a kid, but then I couldn't remember the name of it."

Señora P turned around. "It is the same pool that is there now, to this day. Shelby Pool: the home of the Sharks. You know it because you go there too."

"Ah," I said. "Good point. Thanks for the clarity. I thought maybe it had changed names over the years."

"That surely does happen," Mrs. Silvers said. "And I know the pool well. Used to work at the snack bar, I did. And could I swim."

"Could you?" Darbie asked.

"Quite well."

"Could *you*?" Hannah asked Señora Perez.

She chuckled. "I was not very good. I liked to stay where I could stand."

On that, Mrs. Silvers stood. "I think it's time for me and Elvis to go."

"Okay. I'll take you," Darbie said.

"I can do it, Darbie, but thank you, and thank you for the music machine. I like it."

"You're welcome," Darbie said. Then her phone vibrated

in her pocket. She pulled it out. "Yay! It works again!"

Mrs. Silvers walked toward the door with hardly any limp at all, and then she turned back. "I almost forgot to give you this." She took an envelope out of her sweater pocket and handed it to me. "It's mail that came to my house for your mom. I guess with the similar house number and our initials being the same and all, it's easy to get us mixed up."

"My mom's initials are BQ," I said.

"Well, like you said, names change. Mine used to be Regina Wright, but when I married, it became Silvers. Your mom used to be Becky Smythe, before she married." She added, "You'll give this to her? It looks like an important invitation."

"Of course," I said.

Mrs. Silvers and Elvis left the building.

Darbie asked, "For a second I thought she meant your mom was RS."

I held up the envelope addressed to Rebecca Smythe Quinn. "Becky is short for Rebecca," I said. "It's a family name."

"RS," Hannah said slowly.

We heard Señora Perez giggle as the beaded curtain swung closed.

29

Road Trip

The next day I asked, "So, Mom, when are you leaving for your reunion?" at the same time I texted Tony the recent RS intel.

He replied, **It was your mom all along and you didn't know it?**

"Tomorrow around eleven. I'm taking the noon train," Mom said. "Why?"

Yeah, I responded to Tony. Then to Mom I said, "I was thinking it would be nice for me to see where you grew up." Then I added, "And my friends, too."

Tony asked, **If your mom hid—as in, she didn't want any-**

one to find it—the Book in the attic then why wouldn't she move it when she knew you were cleaning it?

Hmmm.

"That's a great idea, Kell. You can stay with your aunt Aggie while I'm at the reunion. She's been dying for you to visit. When I tell her that you and your friends want to see what Salem is like during Halloween, she is going to be delighted!"

"Aunt Aggie doesn't eat, right?"

Mom sighed. "Don't exaggerate. She eats. She's vegan. It's very healthy for you."

"And she would be okay if I brought friends?"

"The girls? Sure. She'd love it."

"And how about the Rusamano twins?"

"The more the merrier." Then she added, "I'll just give her a call." Before dialing, she said, "You might want to tell Darbie to pack snacks, just to be safe."

I texted the girls and the Rusamanos, **It's a go. Meet at my house tomorrow at eleven.**

Then I texted just the girls, **What about CB? We can't go away and leave her entranced.**

Darbie texted, **Sure we can.**

Hannah's text was more helpful, so I called Charlotte to come over.

She knocked on the back door. I opened it and said, "Come in." She didn't say anything sassy like she usually does when I open the door for her. I said, "Charlotte, I want you to delete the videos and pictures of the Book from your phone.

She did exactly what I said. Man, I loved Memory Maker Part Two. I was going to miss it.

Then I took out a Moon Honey drop that we'd gotten from Señora P that morning. "Eat this." I commanded.

After she finished, she looked startled, like she had no idea what was going on.

"Kelly Quinn!" she yelled at me. "You . . . what are you doing? What was I saying?"

I helped her out, "You think that I'm not good at soccer, or . . . anything, actually."

"Yeah. You should take it more seriously, like Hannah. If you trained and practiced like me, there could be hope for you."

"You're probably right. You go on home, and I'm gonna have a long think about that."

Just then my mom came into the kitchen. "Hi, Charlotte," she said. "It's so nice to see you two finally hanging out together."

"Oh, I know!" Charlotte said. "In fact, I was just telling Kelly how we need to train for soccer together."

"That's a good idea," Mom agreed. "Bring a ball with you this weekend, and you can kick it around."

"Uh, Mom . . ."

"This weekend?" Charlotte asked.

"To Salem. We're going. You should totally come with us," Mom said.

"Oh, Mom, Charlotte wouldn't like that. She is much too busy with important things to do. You know, she has student council, and she's popular, and all that. And," I said to Charlotte, "my aunt Aggie is a little weird." I twirled my finger outside my ear. "She's a vegan." I stuck a finger into my mouth.

"Actually, that all sounds great. I'm always looking for ways to improve my health," Charlotte said. "And for once, I'm free this weekend!"

"Excellent. And maybe you can rub some of your healthy habits off on Darbie," Mom said.

"I can try, Mrs. Quinn, but she's a tricky one, that rascal."

"Don't I know it,'" Mom said. "Do you know what she does to my M&M's?"

"Only too well."

Mom said, "We're leaving for the train at noon, so you better get packed up. I can talk to your mom about the trip, if she wants."

"No need. If you're going, she'll be fine with it. She thinks you're a model mother, Mrs. Quinn."

My mom blushed, and I rolled my eyes at Charlotte's blatant brown-nosing.

"I'll bring my sneakers, for sure, so I can jog in the early a.m."

Mom said, "Kell, *that's* not a bad idea."

"Super," I mumbled.

Charlotte bopped out the back door, and Mom went upstairs.

I texted the girls that Charlotte was coming with us for the weekend, to search in a tomb for a letter about the rules of the magic of our Secret Recipe Book.

How did that happen? Hannah texted.

Luckily, I didn't have to answer because Darbie wrote right back with, **What's the deal with the food?**

Just pack yourself plenty of snacks, I responded.

On it, Darbie replied.

As I waited for the rest of my friends (and Charlotte) to arrive, I thought about Tony's question while I flipped through an album of old photos mom had left on the counter. There were pictures of her high school graduation, in 1996. I doodled math on a napkin—Hannah could've done it in her head. My mom wouldn't have even been born in 1959, so she couldn't be our RS.

Were we headed on a wild RS chase?

30

When in Salem

We took the Acela out of downtown Wilmington and headed north. Even though we pretty much ate for five whole hours the entire way there, we didn't even dent Darbie's stash of food: summer sausages, beef sticks, and canned hash—which sounds gross but is de-lish!

We got off the train at the Salem stop (Mom went one stop farther to her reunion in Danvers) and stepped onto the platform to search for Aunt Aggie.

"Um," Hannah said. "This could be difficult."

We were just a week and a half from Halloween, and

Salem takes Halloween very seriously. So people start dressing up early. We had to find Aggie among the sea of elaborate costumes, masks, and really impressive made-up faces.

I walked through the crowds of people in the train station and tried to give everyone a close look without being too creepy or rude, but Darbie was the one who found her by dragging her suitcase around calling "Aunt Aggie? Aunt Aggie!" like a lost puppy.

Not two seconds later I heard, "Yoo-hoo! Kelly!" And then I saw her familiar smile. Aggie was tall and slim and a few years younger than my mom. She was dressed in a black shirt and leggings with a long black velvet cape with purple satin trim thrown over her shoulders. She was wearing a pointed witch's hat that was dolled-up with purple boa feathers, and she had purple rhinestones in the corners of her eyes.

"You look great," I said to her.

"When in Salem . . ." She spread her arms and twirled so that we could take in the whole getup, complete with the purple high heels.

She grabbed me into a big hug. And then each of my friends. Charlotte stood stiffly when Aggie's arms wrapped around her. "Oh," Aunt Aggie said, "we'll have to work on you!"

"Wow," Hannah said, looking at Aunt Aggie and me. "You two could be sisters."

"I know!" Aunt Aggie said. "Can you believe it? And I'm not even really her aunt."

"You aren't?" Frankie asked.

"No. I am her mom's cousin. I guess that would make me your second aunt, or second cousin. Oh, who knows and who cares. Family is family."

She looked at my friends. "Let me guess. You're Charlotte," she said first. "And you're Darbie." She nudged Darb with her elbow. "I've been warned about you. But I've completely stocked the house with M&M's and separated all the colors for you."

"I like you already," Darbie said happily.

"And you're Hannah. And the Rusamano twins. Hmm, I expected you to look more alike. Are you sure one of you wasn't switched at birth?"

"Everyone says that," Tony said, then whispered to Aggie, "I look more like my parents. Just sayin'."

"Well, I won't have any trouble keeping you straight. You're Tony, and you're Frankie." She was right on the first guess. "I received quite an amazing package from your mom this morning.

"How did she get it here so fast?" I asked.

"She's a woman of many talents," Frankie said. "Moving

food from one place to another is an easy one for her."

"Now I don't have to cook all weekend, which is great because I want to show you so so so many things, and I want to tell you all about Salem. But the way you look—it simply won't do."

An hour later we were outfitted to fit in with Salem Halloween culture. Frankie and Tony were pirate ghosts, Darbie was a pilgrim ghost, Hannah was a zombie, I was a ghostly clown, and Charlotte was a devil.

Aunt Aggie studied us outside the costume store. "Much better. Now, where should we start?"

"Well," I began "there is something that we—"

"I know!" Aunt Aggie exclaimed.

31
Mac

As anxious as I was to get to the Salem cemetery, how could we say no to ice cream? And, frankly, I was a little nervous about what Darbie would do to me if I said no to ice cream.

"I don't eat ice cream myself," Aggie said after we'd loaded into a minivan that comfortably fit seven people with luggage, although we had to tie Darbie's suitcase to the roof. "But there's a place I've driven past that maybe you'll like." She pointed out a few sites, including the Witch Trials Memorial and the Ropes Mansion.

Aunt Aggie slowed down and pointed out a large, dark

house with a few chimneys. "There's the famous House of the Seven Gables. It has a closet with a false back that leads to a secret staircase just like in Nathaniel Hawthorne's famous novel." A second later she announced, "Here we are. The Frosty Cow." It was two stores down from Count Orlok's Nightmare Gallery. When Frankie saw it, he said, "I totally want to go there. I heard that during October the monsters in the museum come to life."

"Monsters?" Charlotte asked. "I'll pass."

"I'll stick with the Frosty Cow," Darbie said. "I never met ice cream I didn't like."

Aunt Aggie dropped us off at the door. "I'm going to fill up with gas, and I'll be there in a minute."

We were the only customers in the Frosty Cow. There was a worker, dressed like Freddy Krueger, who sat behind the counter flipping through a lacrosse magazine.

"You play?" Frankie asked him. I swear, he could talk with anyone.

"Yup. You?"

Frankie nodded and held up a fist to bump like the two were now on the same team.

"The name's Mac," he said. "What can I get you?"

"Why does your name tag say it's Evan?" Darbie asked.

"It is, but everyone calls me by my middle name because my dad is Evan also, and it gets confusing."

"Gotcha, Mac," Darbie said. "Can I taste a flavor or two before I commit?"

"Sure. That's what these tiny spoons are for."

"Great. Can I try strawberry, mint chocolate chip, banana peanut butter, French vanilla, butter pecan, cookie crunch—"

Mac scooped tiny spoons of each flavor before she even had the names out of her mouth.

"Rum raisin, oatmeal, moose tracks—"

"Darb," I said. "Why don't you start with those?"

"Fine."

Darbie licked nearly every spoon clean. Mac asked, "So, what will it be?"

"I'll have strawberry and French vanilla blended with cookie bites, brownie bites, Twizzler bits, and Skittles, with whipped cream, rainbow sprinkles, and a cherry on top. I call it the Rocket Launching Rainbow Super Swirley."

"Well, it sounds great, except we don't have half of those toppings."

"What?!" Darbie was shocked and appalled by the announcement. "What don't you have?"

"The Twizzler bits and Skittles. And we ran out of the brownie bites."

Tony said to Darbie, "Just get that other stuff on top and let someone else order."

"No way." She looked at Mac. "I'm about to make your day!"

"Oh really?"

Aunt Aggie pulled up out front and looked like she was talking on the phone.

"Tony?" Darbie asked. "Do you think you can get my suitcase from the van?"

"If you'll leave this guy alone so he can take care of us other paying customers?"

"Deal."

Tony left.

Frankie placed his order for vanilla ice cream with whipped cream and examined the cup when Mac handed it over. "Kind of boring, huh?" Frankie asked.

Mac shrugged. "I don't care what you order. I just work here."

Tony came in with the big rolling bag and handed it to Darbie.

She rolled it behind the counter. "Buckle up," she said. "I'm about to rock your world."

Mac asked the boys, "Should I be worried?"

"I think you probably should let her go. Stopping her could be hazardous to your health," Frankie said.

"All right." Then he asked Tony, "What can I get you?"

Tony asked Frankie about his. "How's that?"

"Eh."

"I guess I'll have that," Tony said, indicating Frankie's boring cup.

Darbie made a racket, taking things out of her case and firing up the blender.

"Kell? Hannah-Hasselhoff-Hideaway? I need some backup here," Darbie called to us.

She put me in charge of the ice cream's "presentation," so I inventoried the available sundae glasses, bowls, and stemware and picked just the right ones. I set them on plates that I'd lined with paper doilies. Meanwhile, she sent Hannah to scoop the flavors she needed.

"What should I do?" Charlotte asked, looking unsure if she should join us behind the counter.

"You can just hang out," Darbie said. "I think it's under control."

"How about if I write down the names of the dishes? Like signs. I can write bubble letters, or block or calligraphy. . . ."

"Um," Darbie said. "Okay. That's a good idea."

Mac made himself a bowl of ice cream and sat with Frankie and Tony at a table with a good view of our work. They chatted about sports, Delaware, the train, lasagna, and *Turd Wars*, and watched us.

A few minutes later Darbie loaded seven tall parfait glasses layered with colors and combos of toppings onto a tray and brought it over to the table.

"Taste test time," I said.

"My favorite time!" Darbie said.

"Okay. What have we got?" Hannah asked, laying a bunch of tall spoons on the table.

Darbie provided a description of each layered concoction. "This is pumpkin and cinnamon ice cream with crushed graham crackers, a layer of mini marshmallows, and caramel drizzle."

Charlotte put a paper down next to it, written on in colorful pencils that she'd found. She said, "It's called Autumn Harvest."

Darbie looked closely at Autumn Harvest and asked, "What's that dust?"

"I might have sprinkled the tiniest dab of nutmeg," I said.

"Because you just happen to have nutmeg in your pocket?" Mac asked.

Hannah pointed out, "Kelly always has a dab of nutmeg in her pocket."

Darbie described the next few as we slid in our long spoons and tasted each.

At one with varying shades of brown, Mac asked, "What's this?"

"Different, huh?" Darbie said. "You won't find that one anywhere else."

Charlotte put down the sign: DINNER FEAST.

"Ugh." Frankie made a terrible face and spit his taste out in a napkin. "What's in it?"

"Beef stick, mashed potatoes, and a layer of brown gravy."

Everyone who had a spoon headed in that direction pulled it away, except for Mac, who dove in. "I love it," he said. "And I appreciate a girl who loves weird ice cream!"

Darbie beamed with delight.

When Mac finished Dinner Feast, he said, "I have to say, I've never met anyone with a suitcase like that before. You're very prepared."

Darbie had one spoon in her mouth and another dipped into Peanut Twist. "Thanks. No one's ever said that to me before. Some people"—she shot a look at Frankie and Tony—"don't appreciate me."

"So what are you planning to do while you're in Salem?" Mac asked.

"You know," I said. "Halloweeny touristy stuff."

"Just for the record," Charlotte said. "I'm not doing the monster thing."

"Understood," I said.

Mac looked at Charlotte and then Frankie and Tony for an explanation. They both rolled their eyes.

Charlotte said, "I saw that, Tony Rusamano."

Darbie answered Mac's question. "We're gonna look at tombs."

Hannah said, "It sounds creepier than it is."

"Tombs aren't creepy by Salem standards," Mac said.

"We're on a mission," Darbie added.

"We are?" Charlotte asked.

Hannah said, "More like a quest."

"I like quests, and I know my way around," Mac said.

Darbie looked at me. "Can Mac come along?"

"Wait. What quest?" Charlotte asked.

Mac flipped the sign on the Frosty Cow's door to CLOSED, and we piled back in the van.

"Aunt Aggie, meet Mac," I said.

"Actually," Darbie explained, "his name is Evan, but that's confusing with his dad, who is also named Evan, so people call him by his middle name, Mac."

"Sometimes they call me E. Mac. And sometimes, just to be silly, Mac-E."

"Nice to meet you, Mac," Aunt Aggie said. "That's interesting that you and your dad share a first name. In our family, the women share a middle name."

"You do?" Hannah asked.

"Sure."

32

Samantha

Aunt Aggie explained, "Some women change their last names when they get married, so way back somewhere in our family history, the women decided to use the same middle name. Kelly and I, Kelly's mom, grandmother, great-grandmother, Aunt Elizabeth, et cetera, all have Samantha as a middle name."

"How did I not know your middle name was Samantha?" Darbie asked.

"Jeez, even I knew that," Charlotte said.

Aunt Aggie added, "And that's the way women in our

family identified themselves—with their middle name more than their last name.

Darbie said, "So instead of calling you KQ, I should call you KS?"

Hannah asked, "Your mom would still be RS?"

I added, "And so would my *grandma.* Hannah."

Hannah understood what I meant, "*That* makes sense."

"What makes sense?" Charlotte asked.

"I'm lost," Darbie said.

"Don't worry about it," I said, and I gave Aunt Aggie the address I'd researched for the cemetery where my relatives were buried. "It's all coming together."

Mac, who sat in the passenger seat said, "I always wanted an Aunt Aggie."

"Now you have one. Glad to have you along." Then she said to him, "I hope you like graveyards."

"How could I live in Salem if I didn't like graveyards?" Mac asked.

"Did you say 'graveyard'?" Charlotte called from the third row, where she was now sandwiched in between Frankie and Tony. "I'm smooshed back here!"

Each of the boys tried their best to move closer to their window and give her more room.

"That's a tiny bit better."

"Oh good," Aunt Aggie said. "I would just hate it if you were uncomfortable, Charlotte."

"Thank you," Charlotte said, then: "Wait. Was that sarcastic?"

"We don't have sarcasm in Salem," Aunt Aggie said.

Hannah whispered to me, "What are we gonna do about Charlotte?"

"She already knows most of this." I shrugged. "If we need her to forget, we can always make a potion, I guess." Then I added, "Let's worry about it later. I don't want to miss this moment because of Charlotte."

"Here we are," Aunt Aggie said. "Burying Point Cemetery. It's the second oldest cemetery in the country."

My heart sped up. My grandmother's oldest relatives are buried there. We were so close to finding out the last bits about the magic and the Book.

"Wait," Charlotte said. "You *did* say graveyard. This doesn't look safe or . . . Do we even have authorization to be here?"

"You don't have to go if you don't want to, Charlotte," I said. "I don't think Aunt Aggie would mind if you hung out with her for a little while."

Aunt Aggie said, "I don't mind at all."

"No," Charlotte said. "I'm not scared. I just wanted to make sure the proper paperwork has been completed so that we don't get in any trouble."

The gang tumbled out of the car like a jamboree of circus clowns. I was the last. Aunt Aggie grabbed my wrist. "I'm really proud of you for figuring all of this out."

She surprised me.

"How did you know?"

She pointed to her head under her pointy hat. "We Samanthas have a sixth sense about some things."

"We do?"

She giggled. "Nah. Grandma told me about the Book. I always wanted to see it. You found it, didn't you?"

"Yeah. It's great. I can show it to you later."

As I was about to hop out of the van, she tugged me back. "What is it?" I asked.

"This could be life changing."

"Life changing?"

"Once you dig things up, you can't put them back. Are you ready for that?"

"I don't think I have a choice. It's not like I just *want* to know. It's like I *have to* know. I couldn't stop myself if I wanted to."

"Then, good luck. I live a few houses down the street. Walk there when you're done; I'll drop you a pin." She added, "I'll get your stuff all set up. Take your time."

I leaned over to hug her. "Thanks, Aunt Aggie. Thanks for understanding."

I jumped out.

Tony asked me, "Everything okay?"

"Yeah," I said. "It's great."

We stood out front of what looked like the world's oldest wrought-iron gate, which was covered with vines that had died in the chilly autumn air. The moon was low in the night sky. It wasn't quite full, but bright enough to light our way through the slips of clouds that were out.

"Go on, Kelly Samantha Quinn," Charlotte said.

Tony took my hand. "I'll go with you." He pushed the gate open. It let out a high-pitched screech that I felt in my bones.

"Will you be Shaggy?" Darbie asked Mac.

"I'm so Shaggy."

Hannah said, "Frankie, Charlotte, and I will take the perimeter. Kelly and Tony, check out over there. And, Darbie and Mac, comb the rows in the middle."

"What exactly are we looking for?" Charlotte asked.

Frankie said, "A tomb."

"Duh," Charlotte said. "How silly of me." I could actually *feel* her sarcasm.

"You know," Darbie said to her, "you might have fun, if you tried."

Charlotte dropped her hands from her hips and huffed. "Fine. I'll try."

"Really?" I asked.

"Really," she said in a very un-Charlotte-like tone that made me think she meant it.

We divided up.

"How could a letter be hidden inside a solid headstone?"

Tony wondered. "A crypt makes more sense."

"They don't have crypts or mausoleums here," I said, sharing some of my online research.

We walked along for a while looking at the names. "Would you rather spend eternity under a gravestone or in a cement house?" He was always more talkative when it was just us.

"I never thought about it. I guess it would be nice to be in the cement house with other people close by."

"I think so too."

He looked on the right side of the row, and I looked left.

"Look at that." He pointed to what was clearly a crypt. In fact, there were three. They were tucked, nearly hidden, by trees, adding extra spookiness that I didn't need.

"I guess Mrs. Eagle was right, you can't believe everything you read online."

"Hathorne." He stated the name over the door of a crypt. "He was one of the witch trial judges."

"How do you know that?"

"I may have read about it before coming." He read the second one. "Bishop. Bridget Bishop was a victim of the witch trials. Did you ever read *The Crucible*?"

I heard Tony start talking about Abigail Williams, but his voice faded into the background as all of my attention focused on the third and final crypt. The big, block letters carved in the cement: SMYTHE.

33

The Power of Three

Tony doubled back to where I was standing and stared at the name. "You okay?" he asked.

"I guess. I have chills."

"Me too," he said.

I peeled my eyes from the letters to look at him. "I'm glad you're here."

"Me too," he said again.

For half a second I thought he might . . . I mean, probably not, but I thought maybe . . . he could possibly . . .

"You found it!" Frankie said, hip-checking Tony.

Tony and I jumped apart.

"What are you waiting for, Kelly Quinn?" Charlotte asked.

For once, Charlotte had a point.

They stayed where they were as I pushed the door to the crypt open. It was dark inside, but a bright light emerged over my shoulder. Tony was behind me using his cell phone flashlight app.

I walked in. The floor was surprisingly swept free of dirt, dust, or leaves. There was a stone bench in the middle of a room a little smaller than my bedroom. On each wall there were compartments dedicated to a different person and several ledges that I guessed people would put flowers on, but there were none. The cubbies were marked with a name and date of birth and death. The most recent person who had died was Rebecca Samantha, 5/17/47–4/13/03.

My throat choked a little as I said, "My grandmother."

Tony said, "She was not even fifty-six years old when she died."

"I wish I'd met her. I have so many questions that she'll never be able to answer."

"No. But she left you a letter," Tony said. "That's something."

I looked around the crypt for someplace a letter could be hidden. I ran my hands along the walls and in the crevices. When I didn't see anything, I sat on the stone bench, wrapping my hand on the seat. The very tip of my finger brushed against something. I reached down, and there was a paper inside a plastic bag secured to the underside of the bench with duct tape. No one would ever find it unless they were looking for it. I really had to work to get it off.

"Hey, guys," Darbie called into the crypt.

Then Hannah said, "What's going on in there?"

"She found the letter," Tony said.

The girls came in, followed by Mac, Frankie, and Charlotte.

Charlotte asked, "Letter? Why do I feel like there is a whole lot of backstory here that I don't know?"

Darbie said, "Because there is. Did you ever think we don't include you and don't tell you things because we don't trust you to keep a secret?"

"Well, Darbie O'Brien, did you ever think that I tell those secrets *because* you don't include me?"

"No," Darbie said. "I never thought of that. I thought it was just because you're mean."

For once, Charlotte had nothing to say.

Frankie said, "Can we talk about that stuff later?"

"Yes, focus, people!" I agreed. Then I unfolded the letter, and everyone stood around me and listened to me read:

"The Power of Three:

"In the summer of 1959 I met two friends with whom I wrote a very special book of recipes. These recipes were extraordinary in that they were potions. We conducted many experiments and learned that special ingredients from the Island of Cedros gave the recipes their power. I took special note of when the potions worked and when they didn't and discovered a common denominator that only I knew: The recipes only worked when my two friends and I did them together. There had to be three of us. We made a pact to keep this rule of magic secret. I was never good at keeping secrets, and I couldn't let this information die with me, so I hid this rule of magic in this letter, only to be discovered after my death.

"From, R.S."

"That's it," Hannah said. "That's totally it. The potions that didn't work were the ones we made alone."

"We didn't have the Power of Three for those," I said.

Darbie said, "There are three of us; there were three of them."

I nodded. "The encyclopedia volume was *Volume T* for three; your soccer number is three; mine is six; Hannah's is nine; Memory Maker is a three-part potion. Threes are everywhere."

Hannah said, "It's been all around us."

I said, "It's like she was trying to tell us the whole time, but we didn't see it."

Charlotte said, "People try to tell you a lot of things, but you never seem to see it unless it's right in front of you."

34

Aunt Aggie's Big Secret

We sat in Aunt Aggie's backyard around her fire pit.

"I am so full," Darbie said. "I love lasagna. And I love your mom," she said to Frankie and Tony. "Is it possible she's my fairy food godmother?"

"On puh-lease, Darbie O'Brien, we have potions and powers and magic and now fairy godmothers? Next you'll be waiting to go on an expedition to find leprechauns." And Charlotte did something strange—she giggled. This was a typical sassy Charlotte comment, but she said it in a completely different way than ever before. The giggle wasn't rude and mocking of Darbie, it was just . . . an actual, genuine kind of teasing the three of us do. She had made a joke for fun, not to be horrible, like usual.

Then, to top it off she added, "I'll check the weather app, and tomorrow we can start searching for rainbows. A true expedition. Who's in?"

Darbie said, "We don't have to have an expedition for that. We can lure them in with gold. Those characters are always on the hunt for gold."

"If that doesn't work, we can try baiting them with this lasagna," Charlotte said.

And we all laughed.

This was unlike anything I'd experienced with Charlotte Barney since before my surprise ninth birthday, when she'd spoiled the surprise.

It was truly a magical night.

I put the last of the dishes in the sink while Aunt Aggie washed them. "So now you know. How do you feel?" she asked.

"Good, I guess, but something still isn't adding up."

"What's that?"

"If it takes three girls and ingredients from Cedros to make potions, why didn't anyone else ever figure that out? I mean, that's not rocket science."

"What exactly did the letter say?"

"It explained the Power of Three—that there have to be three girls to make a potion work."

"Then Grandma hadn't figured it all out," Aggie said.

I asked, "There's more?"

"Kind of a biggie."

35
Witch Blood

re you going to tell me?"

"Follow me." Aunt Aggie wiped her hands on a towel and walked down a hallway and opened a big, heavy, wood door. Inside she lit candle sconces on the walls, one at a time as she walked around the room, until we were circled by them. They illuminated the rows of shelves built right into the room's woodwork. In the center was a round table with an ancient-looking book. Aunt Aggie blew dust off its leather cover and opened it, careful not to crack its already fragile binding. Every page contained a handwritten list of names.

I recognized some of them from the history lesson that Tony had given me earlier in the cemetery. "Are these the names from the witch trials?"

"No. The witch trials weren't really about witchcraft. It was a political thing to show power. Most of the people who were put to death weren't witches at all."

"Then what are those names?"

"At the same time as the famous witch trials, there were real witches in Salem. Hiding. A few of them got caught up in the trials, but most remained under the radar."

I finished her thought. "This is a list of the real Salem witches."

She nodded.

"And their descendants."

She nodded again. "Every generation the powers have faded a bit, I think."

She pointed to a name: Rebecca Samantha Charlesworth.

"The Rebecca Samanthas in this book are related to us," I said, not a question, because I was starting to understand. Does my mom know this?"

"I don't think so," Aunt Aggie said.

"If she did, she would've named me Rebecca too?" I asked.

"That's what I think," Aunt Aggie said. "So, do you see what I'm telling you, Kelly?"

I nodded. "That my grandmother, and mother, had inherited witch blood—only my mom never knew it. That all of the female descendants of the Rebecca Samanthas have . . . special abilities?

"Exactly . . ." She added, "All of the RSs and their children, even if they aren't named Rebecca Samantha."

I stared at her until I realized what she was trying to say.

"Me?" I asked.

36

Memory Maker Part Three

You," Aunt Aggie said. "You're special."

I shook my head. "I like the idea of being special, but it also feels like a big responsibility."

"You can handle it," she said. "The actual powers, like I said, have faded over time, but still have that spark for just when it's needed."

I wondered out loud. "Should I tell my friends?"

"That's up to you. I don't think Grandma ever put all the pieces together, and I don't think she ever told the other girls. I would guess she didn't want them to treat her differently."

"That's how I'm feeling too, but I've never kept a secret from Hannah and Darbie before."

"You're lucky to have such good friends. Not everyone has that." She gave me a peck on the top of my head and went to say good night to the girls. But I didn't sleep much.

We woke up and found a note from Aunt Aggie on the counter.

Gang,
I went to yoga. I'll be back in time to take you to the train station.

Kelly,
I left ingredients for you to make a special breakfast. The kind that will give you three times the memory you ever thought you needed.

Xo, Agg

I knew she had written in code about Memory Maker Part Three. There was no recipe for Memory Maker Part Three in my book, so I wondered how Aunt Aggie could have had it. This made me think that maybe she had more potion-related knowledge than she'd told me so far.

I looked at the ingredients on the counter: White bread,

butter, salt, and Cedronian black pepper. The black pepper was in a green glass bottle. There was a Post-it: *Eggs are in the fridge.*

I took out the egg carton. It was full because Aunt Aggie didn't eat eggs. Inside was the handwritten recipe for MM3: Memories in an Egg Pocket. The recipe was signed, RS. I knew what an egg pocket was because my mom had made them. I turned the recipe over. *Feed someone an alternate memory.* That sounded like a great way to manage Charlotte.

I put a frying pan on the stove and remembered that I couldn't do this alone. I woke up Darbie and Hannah and told them I needed their help with breakfast.

Hannah hopped up, but Darbie took more coaxing.

"I'll make you coffee with chocolate sauce and Aunt Aggie's almond milk," I said.

"Ohhh. That sounds good. I would probably be able to move my feet to the floor if I could actually smell it brewing."

"Fine," I said.

I whipped up the steamy mug, brought it in to her, and let the scent float under her nostrils. She rose from her bed and followed the cup as I led her into the kitchen. I sat her down on a kitchen stool and let her sip the cup.

"What are we doing?" Hannah asked.

"Charlotte," I said.

"You know," Hannah said. "She's been kind of nice these last two days."

"I think so too, but she's seen a lot, and I don't think we can let her take all that info back to Wilmington. It's just too risky," I said.

Darbie said, "The first time she gets mad at us for something, which could happen anytime for any reason, who knows what she'd do?"

"Okay," Hannah agreed. "But nothing like Memory Maker Part Two, that was too much."

"Aunt Aggie left me this." I held up Memories in an Egg Pocket. "It looks less hexy than the lotion." I explained how it would work. We'd make the egg pockets together, but only add the Cedronian black pepper to Charlotte's. Then, while we ate it, we would feed her new memories about the weekend that would override the actual ones. When we were done eating, the reprogramming would be done.

"Who's gonna take the Return?" Hannah asked.

"Not it!" Darbie yelled.

"Shh!" Hannah said. "You'll wake her up before we're ready."

"I think you've had your share, Darb. It's my turn," I said.

Hannah warned me, "We don't have any deeds here, so whatever the Return is, you'll have it all the way back to Wilmington."

"Yup. I understand," I said.

I melted the butter in the frying pan, tore a circular hole in a slice of bread, and dropped it into the pan. I flipped the bread a little, and once it was golden buttery, I cracked an egg into the hole and let it bubble. I sprinkled salt and flipped it. I did the same thing with the rest of the bread and eggs. Hannah put the pockets on plates with strawberries and orange slices and set the table. On one we sprinkled Cedronian pepper, and normal pepper on the others.

"Before the boys wake up, I want to tell you girls something," I said. "Because we don't keep secrets from each other."

I explained about the history of my family.

"You're a witch like a real wart-on-the-nose, green-faced, melt-from-a-bucket-of-water kind of witch?" Darbie asked.

"No," I said. "Not like that. I'm a descendant, which means I might sometimes have just a little spark when it's really needed. And when I'm with the two of you of course, you know, three and all." Then I added, "So we'll have to be best friends forever."

"Forever," Hannah said.

"And ever," Darbie added.

Frankie walked in the kitchen, "What's 'forever and ever'?" Without getting an answer, he hung his nose over the plates "That smells good," Frankie said.

"So good." Tony came into the kitchen. His hair was all mussed up from sleeping; it was so cute.

We explained which egg pocket was for Charlotte and how the potion worked, and Tony went to get Charlotte.

Frankie was pouring orange juice when Tony ran back into the kitchen.

"She's gone."

37

Joe Barney for Mayor

Gone?" I asked.

"Can you clarify?" Hannah asked.

"As in, not in her bed."

One second later the front door opened, and in walked sweaty Charlotte. "Now you sleepyheads are up."

"Where were you?" Frankie asked.

"I went for a morning run. Like always." Then she added, "What? Were you worried about me?"

"We just didn't want to eat breakfast without you." I held out the chair by her peppered pocket. "Sit down." She did, and everyone else followed suit.

"Oh, that's nice. I'm starving." She dug right in, and we started talking.

"That water park was awesome," Frankie said. "I love the lazy river."

Darbie said, "And how about that haunted house? I was so scared."

And just like that Charlotte was fed the details about a completely different weekend, equally full of fun.

To make sure it was working, I asked Charlotte, "Remember the water park and haunted house?"

"Totally," she said. "They were great."

And Darbie said, "And I worked out with you every day and I ran faster than you and you finally believed me that I can tell M&M colors apart based on their taste."

"You're faster than I thought, and you truly have a gift for M&M's," Charlotte agreed.

Memory Maker Three had been a success.

I made it back to Wilmington without a Return finding me. But that's the thing about Returns, they getcha when you least expect it. So I was on high alert.

We regrouped with Señora Perez, who had already started packing up the store.

"This seems a little premature, Señora P," Hannah said.

Darbie picked up a colorful scarf from the hook on the wall. "Can I have this?"

Señora P nodded at Darbie.

"Cool beans." Darbie whisked the silky scarf around her neck.

"You girls do not worry about me. Now tell me, did you find the letter?"

"We did," I said.

Darbie added some color. "It was literally in a crypt. Like *inside*. Kelly was so brave—she went in and got it. Oh, and *Tony* went with her. I saw them holding hands."

"Then you have very much to tell me."

"We're just friends," I said.

The three of them exchanged a look like they knew I was lying.

I thought maybe we were starting to be a little more than friends, but it wasn't anything to put words around yet. I ignored their looks and kept going.

"The letter explained the Power of Three," I said to change the subject, and explained to her that all three of us needed to make a recipe for it to work. I left out the part where one of the three had to be me, and that my ancestors were witches who managed to escape the witch trials. It sounded crazy in my head. Would she even believe me? It hadn't even really sunk in with me.

"*Tres*," she said. "That makes sense. Throughout history, three has always been a magical number. The best things come in threes. It forms a triangle. We describe time in threes: past, present, and future; beginning, middle, end. In many cultures and religions three is a number of rituals. In tales, the hero is always granted three choices or three wishes. And all colors come from the primary three."

"I never noticed all of that," Hannah said.

Darbie's phone chirped with a text. I jumped at the sound, thinking it could be my Return.

"Why so jumpy?" Señora P asked.

Hannah said, "She's waiting for a Return. We used Memory Maker Three on Charlotte, and Kelly added the Cedronian pepper. She hasn't gotten a Return yet."

"Ah. I understand."

Darbie held up her phone. "It's Mac again. He's so funny." She showed us a selfie Mac took of himself with straws stuck under his top lip like a walrus.

The shells hanging on the store's front door jingled, and in walked Mr. Barney. He looked around the store. "Are you going to be done in time?"

"In time for what?" I asked.

Señora P said softly, "To be out by the end of the month."

"The end of *this* month, as in by Halloween? Like in two days? I thought you had another month?" Hannah asked.

Señora P shook her head. "This way I do not have to pay the new rental rate for November."

Darbie stared at Mr. Barney, and I was sure she was going to say something terrible to him. Instead she asked, "Have you ever thought of running for mayor?"

38

The Return Found Me

*M*ayor?

I mean, he was kicking Señora P out of her store, and Darbie was talking local politics?

Then she added, "Because you would be great. Seriously, exactly what this town needs."

Mr. Barney stood up a little straighter. "Why, yes. I've been thinking about it, actually. I'm preparing to announce any day. How in the world did you know?"

"People are always surprised by how perceptive I am."

She was right about that.

"Since when are you interested in local politics?" Hannah asked Darbie.

"Since Mayor Marini announced he wouldn't run for reelection, I've been looking carefully at the elders of our community to see who'd be good for the job."

Mr. Barney started to say, "My campaign would—"

Darbie finished his thought. "—sure be tough if the biggest thing to happen to Wilmington was three girls on TV with the one and only Felice Foudini, telling every voter that you kicked a poor woman out of the store she'd invested her life in. Man, that'd be a bummer." She frowned at the idea. "Wouldn't it, Mr. Barney?"

Darbie was a genius. I may be a secret witch descendant, but Darbie O'Brien was a secret genius!

Hannah picked up on what she was doing and chimed in. "People would not like that. It would really make the election hard for you."

For good measure I added, "Maybe *impossible* to win."

"Oh," he said, looking flustered. "Well, that's not what's happening here at all. The rent for these stores hasn't increased in five years. I'm just going with what the actual rental rate should be now."

"I have an idea, girls," Hannah said. "We could invite the mayoral candidates to come on the show with us. They could cook with us, and people could get to know them. I mean, assuming it's okay with Felice Foudini."

Darbie said, "I'm sure she'd be okay with it. She seems to love Kelly."

"But, we might not have time to have them all on the show, though. . . ." I let that hang out there to see if Mr. Barney would bite.

And he did. "I'll make you a deal," he said. "I won't raise the rent on one condition. Make that two."

"What?" Darbie asked.

He softened his look a bit. "Please invite Charlotte to be on the show with you."

And there it was. The Return. It found me and hit me where it hurt most—my Felice Foudini show.

"Why would she want that?" Darbie asked. "She doesn't even like us."

"That's not true at all," Mr. Barney insisted. "She hasn't stopped talking about your weekend. She especially liked the lazy river. I haven't seen her this happy in a long time."

Mr. Barney paused. "You know, she's always jealous that you have each other. I mean, Kelly, you guys were friends for a while when you were younger. Don't tell her I told you this, but she's wanted to be friends with you girls forever. You started that cooking club and never invited her, even though she was right next door the whole time. She even went over to your house when she knew you were all there, and not once did you ask her to stay."

My eyes met with Darbie's and Hannah's. I knew them

so well that I could read their expressions. Darbie's told me, *Don't agree to it*, while Hannah's said, *Awww, she just wanted to be our friend this whole time.*

"Fine," I said. "She can be on the show, assuming Felice Foudini says it's okay, but she'll have to earn our friendship. You might not believe this, but she hasn't been very nice to us."

"And, maybe, you have not been very nice to her," Señora P pointed out.

Señora P had a fair point.

"What's the second condition?" Hannah asked.

"That I'm the first candidate you have on the show."

"Darbie, what do you think? It was your idea," I said.

"No promises, but we'll work with the producers," she said.

39

The Deed

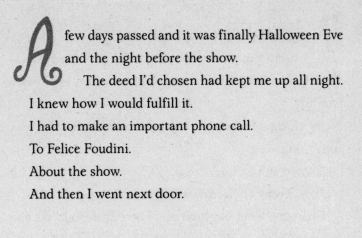few days passed and it was finally Halloween Eve and the night before the show.

The deed I'd chosen had kept me up all night.

I knew how I would fulfill it.

I had to make an important phone call.

To Felice Foudini.

About the show.

And then I went next door.

Back to the
Birthday Party

I knocked on the Barneys' back door.

Charlotte answered and instantly put her hands on her hips. "What do you want to borrow now, Kelly Quinn?"

"Nothing." I changed my mind. "Actually, there is something."

"I knew it."

"You. I want to borrow you. For the TV show."

Charlotte tilted her head and checked me out like she was wondering what I was up to.

"It's like you said in Salem. It was right in front of

me. Or, in this case, next door. You and I have practically grown up together, and we should be friends."

Her mouth gaped in disbelief.

"I mean, if you want to."

She nodded, and after a beat she said, "Kelly, I'm sorry I spoiled your ninth birthday surprise party."

41

Halloween

hree, two, one, and action!"

Felice Foudini walked onto the set that had been temporarily set up in the middle of La Cocina.

When I'd called Felice, she'd loved the idea of having the show in the store. This fulfilled my deed: *Help someone in trouble.*

Señora P was more than "someone"—she was my friend.

Felice thought the store was a little dark and dusty for the image she was trying to present so she sent in a cleaner and an electrician to bump up the lights.

The place looked great.

It kept its antique, old-fashioned charm and maintained its spooky attractiveness, including the moose head. To add to the ambiance, Señora P had her crow sitting nearby, giving the evil eye to everyone on set—and everyone watching at home.

In addition to the camera crew, the store was packed with people: my mom and dad and little brother; Mr. and Mrs. Rusamano; Pete, from the landscaping business; Mrs. Silvers and her daughter Joanne; Mr. and Mrs. Barney; Mr. Douglass and LLJ; Coach Richards and Coach Madden—somehow they had become friends at a coaches meeting while we were in Salem; and Mac and Aunt Aggie, who took the train down from Salem.

"Here I am," Felice said to the camera. "In Wilmington, Delaware, with the winners of my recipe challenge." She waved to us. "Come on out, Kelly."

We walked out to the set.

"Introduce your cooking team."

I said, "We're actually more of a club."

"I love it," Felice said, and flashed her signature smile. "A cooking club. Sounds like something every town should have."

"I couldn't agree more," I said. "The members of the club are: Darbie O'Brien, Hannah Hernandez, Tony Rusamano, Frankie Rusamano, and Charlotte Barney."

"Okay—"

I interrupted the celebrity chef. "And we're filming at the one and only cooking store in the entire region with products sourced directly from Mexico. It has been an inspiration for many of our most wonderful dishes." I held my hands up. "La Cocina!"

"Okay—"

This time Hannah interrupted her. "La Cocina has the best spices in the world."

"And," Darbie added, "if you don't live nearby, you can order them from the brand-new La Cocina website."

Mac gave her a thumbs-up and tapped on his iPad. He'd whipped up a website with shopping features. After the show, everyone watching us was staying to help fulfill orders. And, of course, eat our Brew Stew.

"I have to agree, this place is a hidden gem," Felice Foudini said. "Let's get cooking. What are you making?"

I said, "Charlotte, why don't you tell them?"

Charlotte put on a black pointy hat, and we did the same. "This is a warm and bubbly Halloween treat: Brew Stew."

"Sounds fab!" Felice said. "Take it away."

We walked through the recipe, which we mixed in a big bowl shaped like a cauldron.

Fifteen minutes later, Felice came back on, and we handed her a steamy mug. "It sure does look spooky," she said. "But let's see how it tastes." She took a spoonful.

"Mmmmm. You have to try this. It's so good. Remember,

Kelly Quinn and her cooking club will be on every week coming to you live right from La Cocina."

"And remember," Charlotte said.

We all joined in and yelled, "You. Can't. Be. Too. Yummy!"

Recipes

Have fun making some of Kelly's favorite recipes—but make sure you have a trusted adult helping you out!

Veggie Enchi-La-Di-Das

1 yellow onion, chopped
1 green pepper, chopped
1 package frozen veggie crumbles
1 package frozen chopped spinach
1 28-oz can crushed tomatoes
1 packet taco seasoning mix
16 flour tortillas
1 can or jar enchilada sauce
2 cups shredded cheddar cheese
sour cream (optional)
salsa (optional)
guacamole (optional)

In a saucepan, sauté onions and peppers till softened. Add veggie crumbles and spinach. Mix in pan until everything is hot. Add can of crushed tomatoes and taco seasoning packet. Let cool for ten minutes.

Put several spoons of mixture into a tortilla and roll it up. Place rolled tortillas side by side in a baking dish. Fill dish with tortillas. Pour enchilada sauce over the tortillas and sprinkle with shredded cheddar cheese.

Bake in 350-degree oven for 30 to 40 minutes or until hot and bubbly.

Serve with sour cream, salsa, and guacamole.

Slowpoke Cooker Fettuccine

1½ pounds boneless, skinless chicken breast

2 8-oz packages mushrooms

2 8-oz packages light cream cheese

1½ cups parmesan cheese

2 sticks butter

1½ cups skim milk

1 pound fettuccine

garlic salt

pepper

Put all ingredients except fettuccine in slow cooker.

Cook on low for 4 hours, or high for 2 hours.

Cook fettuccine according to package directions.

Add to slow cooker.

Mix fettuccine and sauce in slow cooker

and let warm through for 20 minutes on low.

Awesome Velvety Red-Carpet Cake with Filling

1 stick butter, melted

4 oz cream cheese, softened

1 cup buttermilk

3 eggs

1 cup premade vanilla pudding

1 tsp vanilla

3 drops red food coloring

1 box butter-flavored cake mix

1 tsp cocoa powder

1 can or jar raspberry or strawberry pie filling

1 can butter or cream cheese frosting

Blend melted butter, softened cream cheese, buttermilk, eggs, pudding, vanilla, and food coloring with a hand mixer. Add cake mix and cocoa powder. Blend thoroughly until the batter is a rich red. Add additional food coloring if necessary. Divide evenly into two greased cake pans. Bake at 350-degrees until cooked through. (Time will depend on your pan; approx. 20 minutes for a 9-inch baking pan.)

Let cakes cool, then remove from pans.

Spread pie filling on top of one cake, then place the second cake on top of the filling.

Cover entire cake with frosting.

Acknowledgments

Recipe for successful writing:

5 crunchy critique partners: John, KB, Jane, June, Chris, Janis, Kathleen, and Greg

1 scrumptious editor: Alyson Heller

1 delicious agent: Alyssa Henkin

3 fabulous children: Ellie, Evan, and Happy

1 understanding hub: Kevin

1 bazillion encouraging family members

A sprinkling of friends who tolerate this life of mine

And the cherries on top: The readers, librarians, and teachers who send me e-mails, letters, pictures, selfies, posts, and Tweets

TURN THE PAGE FOR A LOOK
AT WHERE IT ALL BEGAN.

1

The Secret in the Attic

Question: *What do you get when you mix two girls hungry for cash with a cleaning project?*

Answer: *Kelly Quinn and Darbie O'Brien in a dark, dusty, spider-webby attic on their last day of summer vacation.*

Correction: I, Kelly Quinn, was cleaning. Darbie Rollerbladed in the clutter-free areas, careful not to bang her head on the rafters.

THUD!

I had missed Darbie this summer while she had been at her dad's house at the beach and I had been at camp. "Are you okay?" I asked.

"Fine." Darbie sat among the piles of attic stuff, rubbing her head. "Where did all this junk-arooni come from?" she asked.

"Some of it was my grandmother's. And some belongs

to the witch, Mrs. Silvers, from across the street. Her basement flooded years ago, and presto, we got her junk," I said.

"Are you gonna give it back to her?"

"She says she doesn't want any of it," I said.

Darbie lifted a heavy old book out of a tub full of old books, magazines, and newspapers. "Check out this book. It looks older than my grandpa Stan." She blew off the dust, her skin shining with sweat, and I noticed her freckles were dark from her beach tan. (I never mention her freckles out loud. Last time I did, she Rollerbladed over my sandwich: smoked ham and Muenster cheese, with honey mustard on rye.)

Books are "blah" to Darbie. I don't love them myself, unless it's my journal or one of my cookbooks.

Oh, BTW, I'm Kelly Quinn, age twelve, seventh-grader, lover of all things cooking, mediocre soccer player, average student, and best friend to Darbie O'Brien and Hannah Hernandez.

I wasn't thrilled to spend my last day of summer vacation cleaning the attic. However, I needed the money, and any time I could spend hanging with one of my BFFs couldn't be all that bad.

"Look, Kell," Darbie said excitedly, dusting off a book. "It's dated 1953." For a book to capture Darbie's attention, I figured it must've been something pretty interesting.

"Wow, that's older than my mom." I wiped the rest of the book off with the bottom of my T-shirt. "It's a *World Book Encyclopedia, Volume T.*"

"Encyclopedia? Yuck!" Darbie tossed the book like it was a hot tamale burning her fingers. I was curious, so I flipped through it. I looked for "tamale."

It only took a second for me to realize there was no tamale, tomato, turnovers, or anything else starting with the letter *T*. In fact, the book wasn't filled with anything encyclopedia-ish. The original pages were pasted over with yellowed stationery. The papers were thick, a little crunchy, and stained in places. The words on the stationery were handwritten, a little sloppy, and a few were in Spanish. I knew what I was looking at right away.

These were recipes.

I sat on the trunk and looked at each heavy page. The names of the recipes were very interesting: Forget-Me-Not Cupcakes, Love Bug Juice, and Tell Me the Truth Tea. And there were notes written all around the edges of the stationery, in the margins of the encyclopedia.

"Darbie," I said. "This isn't an encyclopedia at all. It's a bunch of recipes *hidden in* an encyclopedia. Do you know what that makes this?" I asked.

"A recipedia!" Darbie said, grabbing some chunky pearls and bejeweled sunglasses from a hatbox as she Rollerbladed by. "That sounds perfect for a Food Network junkie like you." She was right. I *love* to cook. Ever since my encounter with the famous TV chef Felice Foudini herself, I haven't been able to get enough of cooking. My mom and I cook together all the time, and my other BFF, Hannah, gave me the very first book in my cookbook collection, which consists of six books ranging across the meal, dessert, and snack spectrums. They're stored on a kitchen shelf with different colored Post-it notes sticking out from all sides.

"No, not a recipedia. Listen to this stuff: 'Induces sleep,' 'Keeps 'em quiet,' 'Brings your true *amor*.' Darbie, there's only one thing better than a cookbook, and that's a Secret Recipe Book! And that's exactly what this is."

Just then, the latch on the attic door jiggled. It rattled hard like someone was trying to break in, which was strange because I would've preferred breaking *out*. Suddenly my sweaty mom, who had been cleaning out the garage, tumbled into the attic from pushing the door so hard. She stood at the top of the stairs with a red bandana covering her hair and ears, and yellow rubber dishwashing gloves covering her hands, looking like she'd just appeared on *Extreme Makeover: Dork Edition*. Thank goodness Hannah wasn't here to see the outfit. She's our local fashionista, particularly known for always color coordinating her headband, outfit, and socks.

"Mrs. Silvers just called." Mom sounded frustrated that

Mrs. Silvers had interrupted her cleaning day. "She said Rosey pooped in her yard again. Would you please go over and pick it up?"

Mrs. Silvers is my older-than-dirt neighbor from across the street and she's as nasty as a witch. She's convinced that Rosey, our beagle, flies over, or tunnels under, our fenced-in backyard every day for the sole purpose of pooping in her yard. One day, when Rosey was a puppy, before we had the fence, she actually *did* poop in that yard and Mrs. Silvers saw her. Rosey hasn't left our yard since. Still, thanks to that incident, I scoop for every dog on Coyote Street that uses Mrs. Silvers's yard as their personal bathroom.

While scooping didn't thrill me, I was dying to get out of the hot attic to get some sunlight and fresh air. "Sure," I said, and Mom vanished back down the stairs.

Darbie said, "She looks like she's arming herself to enter a chicken pox colony."

"Unlike you, my mom hates bugs and spiders. She won't touch them. When she cleans, she's afraid they'll land in her hair or crawl into her ears," I explained.

Darbie considered this. I could tell she was thinking about the bug thing.

"Before you ask, no. You can't stay and catch any. Besides, bats and rats hang out in attics, not bugs," I told her.

When our attic work was pretty much done, we headed

across the street to Mrs. Silvers's house. I walked, pooper-scooper in hand, while Darbie Rollerbladed. She blades pretty much everywhere. The crazy thing is that Darbie isn't a great blader. She's an okay blader who just manages to keep herself upright. (Of course, I don't tell her that.) She stumbled to the driveway, to the sidewalk, to the street, to the grass. I held out my arm in case she needed it for balance.

I couldn't get the Secret Recipe Book out of my mind. "Why do you think they're hidden in the encyclopedia?"

"What? The recipes?" Darbie asked.

"Darb, not just any recipes, *secret recipes*."

"Right. Well, they are probably hidden because they're secret."

"Exactly what I was thinking." As we got to the yard I warned Darbie, "Don't look directly into Mrs. Silvers's eyes. You'll turn to stone."

Mrs. Silvers yelled from her front porch, "If I see that mutt again, I'm going to call the pound!" She was surprisingly loud for a woman who looked old enough to be dead. Besides the flabby wrinkles that hung from a face covered in a perpetual scowl, her white hair made her recognizable from miles away. It was short and somehow able to defy gravity by sticking straight up in the air. It reminded me of one of those toy trolls that sits on top of a pencil. And while I assumed she had feet, we couldn't see them under the weird muumuu/housedress thing she always wore.

"Man, Silvers is a grouch-a-saurus," Darbie said under her breath.

"You would be too if you were a hundred years old and bent over all crooked," I said. I didn't actually know how old she was, but a hundred sounded about right.

"Why do you have to scoop the poop?" Darbie asked.

"Since Rosey's mostly my dog, I have to be responsible for her." I mimicked my dad on "responsible for her." "And because, if I don't, I won't get my allowance, which I need to support my Swirley habit." Darbie nodded understandingly. She and Hannah had the habit too.

Super Swirleys were the best milkshakes in Delaware, and possibly the world. They're ice cream and all kinds of other stuff blended into a heavenly frozen concoction. I can't live without them. They were made at Sam's Super iScream, which, luckily, was within walking distance from my house.

After a refreshing breath of mid-Atlantic air, we headed back across the street and entered my house through the garage. We stopped in the kitchen for ice water.

Our vegetable-themed kitchen was my favorite room in the house. The walls were painted artichoke green. Our plates were eggplant purple and stacked nicely in a tall glass-doored cabinet. The wallpaper border was a conga line of dancing carrots, cucumbers, bell peppers, radishes, and mushrooms, all with legs, holding pretty much every kitchen appliance, gadget, and accessory imaginable.

Mom appeared, thankfully sans her protective gear. Her spider-free blond hair was flipped up in a clip. She'd changed into a clean LIFE IS GOOD shirt, gray cotton mini-skirt, and cute sandals: undorked. "If I pretend Darbie isn't wearing Rollerblades in my kitchen, will you girls load all the attic stuff into the minivan?" she asked.

We kept quiet, not excited about loading.

"After that, maybe we'll get you two busy bees a soda."

Silence. *No sale*, as my dad would say.

"Oh, all right. After we drop off all the attic stuff at Goodwill, I'll pay you for your work and treat you to Swirley's." We smiled.

Darbie asked Mom, "Can we maybe meet Hannah-Hoobi-Haha at the pool after her laps?" Darbie loved to add a little jazz to Hannah's name.

Mom said, "I think we can do that."

SOLD to the lady with the minivan!

Darbie and I looked at each other and did our happy dance by swiveling our hips in a small circle and shifting our bodies from side to side. We sang, "Oh yeah. It's your birthday, it's my birthday."

Darbie switched to flip-flops and we loaded the van. I worked quickly because I was anxious to fill my belly with a Super Swirley and read the Secret Recipe Book. When we were done, I stuck the book in a canvas messenger bag that I wore across my chest.

As luck would have it, my little brother, Buddy, tagged along. He was five going on annoying. The only thing good about having Buddy with us was that he couldn't be rummaging through my bedroom and smearing his boogers on the wall. (Seriously, I actually caught him doing it.) Before we were even out of the driveway he was singing "The Wheels on the Bus" painfully loud. Darbie and I put our hands over our ears. As we drove off in the noise-polluted, air-conditioned van, I saw Mrs. Silvers looking out her living room window.

Buddy sang, "ALL THROUGH THE TOWN!"